THE
BURNING
CLASS

THE
BURNING
CLASS

a novel by
LUISA
COLÓN

Cemetery Dance Publications
Baltimore
❧ 2025 ❧

Cemetery Dance Publications
132B Industry Lane, Unit #7
Forest Hill, MD 21050
www.cemeterydance.com

Trade Paperback Edition

ISBN:
ISBN: 978-1-964780-32-0

Cover Artwork © 2025 by Matthew Revert
Interior/Ebook Design/Layout © 2025 by Steven Pajak

Acknowledgments

In memory of H.W.

Thank you to Dan Franklin and Lisa Lebel for your support, I am truly grateful to both of you.

—L.C.

Never Pass by Fire: In firefighting, this rule reminds us never to pass one fire in pursuit of another. When you pass by fire you give it the opportunity to come up behind you, cut off your escape route, and cause big problems. When on an attack team if you encounter fire, you had better address it. Either put it out yourself right now, or make sure someone else is going to do something about it.

— From the New York Firefighters Handbook

Prologue

I have my doll with me the whole time.

I carry it to the restaurant. The big family party is being held in a space that's below street level and has no windows. The restaurant itself is completely empty, which feels strange. We walk through the big room, weaving in between tables, and in the back there's a door that opens to a narrow staircase. I'm clutching my doll with one hand and holding onto my mother with the other as we make our way down the stairs. I can hear family sounds of talking and laughing, and I smell food and cigarettes and the faintly musty scent of a basement.

All the grownups at the party make a fuss over me. They ask me how old I am, and I tell them I'm four years old. I'm a big girl. My parents instruct me to hug one relative after another, and one person pretends to try to take my doll away.

"Can I have your baby?" he says. It's my father's oldest brother, Uncle Gene, who we don't usually see because he lives far away. "It's such a nice baby."

I can feel a nervous half-smile on my face as I say, "No."

Everyone laughs.

After that, I stay close to Uncle Gene. He's not a tall man, and his hair is a dull brown color. His face reminds me of a rabbit's. When he pretended to try to take the doll away, he had a big, warm smile. Then it faded away and his expression has been stern ever since—standing on line at the table where all the food is spread out, fiddling with a cigarette lighter, listening to one of the other relatives talk about a distant relative's sudden death. His wife and their two daughters are there but he barely interacts with them at all. I think if I stick with Uncle Gene, he might smile like that again. So I sit next to him and eat spaghetti, the plate balanced on my lap and the doll stuffed in the crook of my arm. I bring him an ashtray when he asks me to, and the grown-ups laugh and one of them says *Gene always had a way with the ladies*. I stand by his side when a cake is brought out and everyone sings to Cousin Margot. Uncle Gene goes off to have a whispered, smirking conversation with Margot's husband, and I'm starting to feel tired so I sit on the stairs with my doll and watch everyone milling around, smoking, talking, drinking, eating.

Then suddenly Uncle Gene is standing right there, one arm up on the wall, his body angled towards me.

"Is your baby getting tired, Analie?"

I nod at him, feeling that nervous half-smile again, and I'm hoping he smiles back at me. Then he asks me if I want to hear a special secret.

2

I nod again, hoping it's a good secret and not a bad one, not a scary one. He jerks his chin up towards the top of the stairs. "Go upstairs and wait for me, I'll be there in a minute," he says. "I'm gonna grab another drink and then I'll come up and tell you the secret."

No one notices as I go up the stairs and carefully open the door at the top. I find myself in the empty restaurant. It's creepy but the lights are on and I'm glad about that. I make my way around tables and chairs until I reach a fish tank in a corner of the room and I sit down on a nearby chair so I can look at the fish. The table is all ready for people to sit at it and eat—it has a tablecloth and silverware and plates and napkins. I put my doll on the table and feed it imaginary milk from one of the drinking glasses.

"Aw, you're feeding the baby," says a voice, and I turn around and it's Uncle Gene standing right behind me with his hands in his pockets.

"She's hungry," I say. "But she can only drink milk because she doesn't have teeth yet."

"Right," says Uncle Gene. "Where did you get the milk, did you buy it at the store or did you make it for her?" I'm confused, and Uncle Gene can tell. He laughs. There is the big warm smile. "Did you know that mommies make milk for their babies?"

I nod uncertainly. I imagine my mother in the kitchen pouring me a glass of milk. My Abuela makes me something she calls Pink Milk and she won't tell me how she does it but the milk isn't just a pale rose color, it's sweet, too.

Uncle Gene looks over his shoulder and then crouches in front of me.

"You're a smart girl," he says. "And a good girl, too. You

3

have such nice manners. I wish my daughters had manners like you." He's staring at me and I'm waiting for the secret. But he just stares at me so finally I ask him. I ask him what the secret is. "The secret is that I want to give you a special kiss for being a good girl," Uncle Gene whispers. "Can I give you the special kiss?"

I nod. I am holding my doll the entire time.

Afterwards I run down the stairs and back into the packed basement room where the adults have finished the cake. There are leftover crumbs and chunks of it on plates all over the place. I go from one adult to the other and all of them look at me like nothing has happened, nothing has changed. So I think, *maybe nothing has happened. Maybe nothing has changed.* Or maybe they all know something happened and it's okay with them. After all, they let it happen. Uncle Gene comes down the stairs a minute later and strolls into the room, drink in hand. Everyone starts getting ready to leave, putting on coats, saying goodbye. My mother instructs me to hug my relatives again, including Uncle Gene, who no longer has the big, warm smile on his face. Something inside of me hurts when I see his expression. His eyes are cold and they flick over me. He doesn't look like someone who shared a secret, or a special kiss.

At home, I pull out the dusty wooden blocks that I used to play with as a baby, and I build a tower and put my doll on the inside of it and make a roof with the remaining blocks.

Dad is walking by me to get to the kitchen and he stands there for a moment, looking down.

"Are you making a house for your dolly, Analie?"

It's not a house, it's a tower. But I nod. I don't say anything.

I don't want to tell him why the baby has to be in the tower, why she must always stay in the tower.

I.
The Dead Girl

1.

Tenny reminded me of an antique doll that had been thrown away a long time ago, in favor of something newer and shinier. She didn't look cared for or loved and she smelled funny, too—damp, as though the discarded doll had been left out in the rain.

"There's a little girl mooning around the neighborhood, looking for a friend," Abuela had told me. "Her hair is like a rat's nest. Go look for her and see if she wants to play, she seems very lonesome, God bless her." I went downstairs, eagerly—I didn't have any friends where Abuela lived, in Gravesend—and sure enough, she was standing in front of the bodega wearing an oddly old-fashioned romper and holding a satchel, bare limbs long and thin. Her hair was light brown and very curly. Some of it separated into perfect, doll-like corkscrews, but as I got closer, I saw that parts of it were matted and tangled. She had the whitest skin I had ever seen, so pale it was almost tinged with blue.

"My Abuela said to come down here and look for you," I said as a way of starting the conversation, and she smiled uncertainly. "My name is Analie."

"I'm Tenny," she said, in a raspy voice. "What's an a-buel-a?"

"Abuela," I said, and giggled. "It means *grandma* in Spanish. But for a long time I thought it was her actual name. And then I heard my mom call her 'Isabelle' and I was confused."

Tenny laughed too. Her eyes were green, but in one eye, a circle of brown bloomed around the pupil, nearly filling the iris, and making it look like she had two different colored eyes.

"*What's* your name again?" I wasn't sure I'd heard it right.

"People call me Tenny," she said. "My full name is Tenacity."

"That's pretty."

"It's a word. It means determination. My mom says I've always been very determined, even from before I was born."

"My mom says I'm stubborn," I offered. "I'm ten, how old are you?"

"I'm twelve."

We both started to speak at the same time and then said, "Sorry, you first," in unison. "You go," I said, generously.

"Central heterochromia," she said, sounding out the words carefully. "My eyes. I know my eyes are weird. It's a condition. That's what it's called."

"Oh," I said, and then, "Your eyes are neat. I have money, want to buy some candy?"

And that was it. It was so easy to make friends with her. I bought us candy, and we sat on a bench outside Abuela's building, and asked each other questions. Tenny lived in Gravesend with her mother and a fluffy white cat named Aurora, after Sleeping Beauty. She said they had once lived in a big brownstone in Park Slope. It had a lot of rooms and a piano and an art studio with a skylight, because Tenny's father liked to paint. Then he died and they fell on hard times, and moved to a one-bedroom apartment in Gravesend. I told her that I lived with my mother and father in Windsor Terrace, which was a neighborhood about a twenty minute drive from Gravesend, and that we came pretty much every weekend to visit my Abuela.

We were finishing up our candy and I was wondering what would happen next when Tenny's strange eyes flickered over my shoulder and her whole body stiffened. I started to say "What—" but she shushed me and whispered, "Don't turn around. Don't say anything." But of course, I turned around.

A tall, teenaged boy was striding down the middle of the street, taking long steps and—incredibly, because he seemed only a little older than us—smoking a cigarette. Tufts of unusually light blonde hair were sticking out from beneath his baseball cap. As he passed, his brown eyes focused on Tenny and he said, "Whoooooooo" with a smirk and a waggle of his fingers. His brow furrowed slightly when he saw me, and then he was receding into the distance, looking like a totem pole made up of sneakers and jeans, a faded t-shirt, and the cap jammed over that headful of blonde hair.

"Who was *that*?"

"*That* was Corvi Welliver," she said, gazing after him. "He's in high school. Did you think he was cute?"

"How do you know him?"

"He lives on my street," said Tenny proudly. "He's a bad kid."

"Really? How?"

"He's just bad. Everyone says he and his friends burned down the house on Shell Road, cause they do vandalism and play with firecrackers. And he's the *ringleader*."

I was intrigued. Tenny saw it in my face, and eagerly continued. "No one knows *for sure* that Corvi started that fire, but did you know Davey Saxe?" I shook my head no. "Everyone *definitely* knows that on the same day, his nose got blown off because he and Corvi were playing with firecrackers." I shrieked at this, covering my face with my hands, and Tenny giggled. "Did you see how Corvi teased me? My mom says when boys tease me, it means they like me. Corvi and his friends always make spooky sounds when they see me." She laughed. "I don't know why they do! But I like it."

2.

Tenny became my friend in Gravesend. I was happy to have someone my age there, and it made me feel better about going to visit Abuela every weekend. It had been boring for a long time, but Mama insisted on it, and my father went along. There was really no reason for him not to—when we went to Abuela's, he had two women waiting on him instead of one. He ate, drank scotch, watched television, and dozed on the sofa. He was usually too sleepy to drive us home that night, and my mother couldn't drive at all, so we frequently slept over. Abuela had a second bedroom with a cot for me at the foot of the queen-sized bed where my parents would sleep.

I introduced Tenny to my family. She was very polite, and I could tell Mama felt sorry for her. Later, Abuela clucked and commented on Tenny's strange eyes, and then the two of them discussed Tenny's hair, how tangled and tragic it was.

My hair was longer than Tenny's, but Mama and I kept it meticulously clean, combed, and braided. One weekend, my mother made it her mission to comb through Tenny's hair. She used olive oil and she worked through the tangles until tears ran down Tenny's face. "*Bendito*, I'll stop anytime you want," my mother told her. "Why don't you let me take you to the beauty parlor, we'll have your hair cut? They'll make it look real cute." But Tenny didn't want her hair cut off, she wanted it long and beautiful and tended to. It took all day Saturday, and well into the night. "Don't you need to call someone at home, let them know you're safe?" my mother kept asking, and Tenny would say, "It's okay. My mom isn't feeling well today, and I don't want to bother her." By the end of the weekend Mama had done it. Shining from a shampoo but still glossy from all the oil, Tenny's hair had been transformed. I couldn't stop touching it and neither could she. She ran her hands through it, she tossed it over her shoulder, and the damp strands began to spring into coils as they dried. She loved Mama before that, but she adored her afterward.

"Her mother should be doing that," Mama whispered

darkly after Tenny had left to go home, proudly whipping her newly silken curls over her shoulder. "You've met her, Analie. Is she always sick?"

At first, I had thought Tenny's mother, Iris, was just a slob. Their apartment was a small one bedroom a few blocks from Abuela's, and when I went to spend time with Tenny, there were drinking glasses all over the apartment—set down by the ironing board, on the bookshelf, even in the bathroom, with leftover brown liquid that Tenny explained to me was a drink called Running Coke. But when I told Mama, she clucked her tongue. "Ay, she means *rum* and *Coca-Cola*," she explained. "I think the mother has a drinking problem."

After that, it made more sense. Iris spent a lot of time in the bedroom, calling out for Tenny in a plaintive, quavering voice. When she made an appearance—short and thin, with at least six inches of grey roots in her dyed, rust-colored hair —she chain-smoked and sometimes burst into tears out of nowhere. Tenny slept on the couch in the living room. She came and went as she pleased, and as we got older, she starting showing up uninvited both at Abuela's apartment and at our house in Windsor Terrace.

Sometimes she climbed through my bedroom window unannounced while I was doing homework. Other times I would go upstairs and open my door and she would be sitting primly on my bed in one of her strange, old-fashioned dresses, reading one of my books and looking like something out of a nursery rhyme gone wrong. Little Miss Muffett, maybe, or Goldilocks. "Hi, Leelee," she'd say, smiling because she was happy to see me, but uncertain about whether the feeling was mutual. And I wasn't always happy to see her. I complained about it to Mama, who looked worried. "She's got nothing, Analie," Mama would say. "No father, no home life, and she's such a strange-looking little thing. Be kind to her."

I had no idea how anything got done in Tenny's household. Who bought food and toilet paper, and changed light bulbs? My own family moved fluidly, as a unit. We had routines. I wore a school uniform. My father worked, and Mama stayed home and cleaned and cooked and took care of me. On weekends we went to visit Abuela, and as I got older I began doing things on my own, with girlfriends, like going to the park or Coney Island or the movies.

After I told Mama about the Running Coke, and Tenny started showing up at our house unannounced, Mama became uneasy. One Saturday. she took a little walk over to meet Iris. I stayed behind at Abuela's place and we played Go Fish with my father and I beat them both every round.

When Mama came back, she sank silently and ominously onto the sofa.

"Analie," she said finally. "You are never going over there again. Why didn't you tell me they lived like that? *¡Ay, dios mío!* That poor child."

"Is it that bad?" Dad tossed his cards down on the table. "No more, Analie. I'm tired of getting my ass kicked."

"*Hey!*" said Mama and Abuela at the same time.

"They live in a pigsty," Mama went on, murmuring in Spanish as she took her shoes off.

"English, please," said Dad. "I don't want to miss any of *this*."

Mama said *Cyrill, it's not funny*, and Abuela leaned forward eagerly. Finally, someone was going to give *her* some gossip instead of the other way around. As Mama dramatically described Tenny's apartment, I went back in my own mind, wondering why I hadn't considered it all more carefully. I knew, obviously, that Tenny and Iris lived a different kind of life than us, and that it was mostly not the kind of life I would want. I did like how much freedom Tenny had, but at the same time I didn't like it. Tenny ate what she wanted, when she wanted to. She never had to clean up anything. She went a public school, but sometimes cut out and spent the entire day at the library. It was intriguing, the way a dark, tangled forest might be intriguing, but I preferred the neat little lawn of my own home life.

The stove in Tenny's kitchen didn't work; they stored pots and pans in it and used a hot plate for cooking. The apartment always smelled like cat litter, because of Aurora. Little plates decorated with pale pink roses and crusted with remnants of cat food were all over the place. And Iris had kept her late husband's prodigious collection of what she called his "girlie magazines."

"He loved that stuff," she told me soddenly one rainy afternoon when Tenny and I complained there was nothing to do. "For the human form—you know. Go ahead, take a look, you're old enough." I was eleven at the time. I felt sick at the sight of the crumpled *Penthouse* that Tenny pulled out of the big carton under the bed—the woman on the cover was braless, in a skimpy tank top and shorts, legs spread. Her face was lowered and obscured in a way that made it look like she didn't have a head—or that her head didn't matter. "I don't want to see anymore," I said sharply, and Tenny shrugged and said they *were* pretty gross.

I was sure Iris hadn't whipped out the porno collection to show Mama, but Mama was still appalled.

"I told Tenny and that mother this and I'm telling you, Analie. Tenny is welcome to come over here, or visit in Windsor Terrace, but she has to call first. No more showing up, climbing through the window." Abuela tsk-tsked at this.

"Was Tenny okay?" I asked. I was trying to imagine the scene—Iris in her bathrobe with a glass of Running Coke, Tenny looking mortified—but it was difficult.

"She was fine," said Mama succinctly. "What, she's not gonna be fine with it? She doesn't have a choice."

The grown-ups kept on talking, and I got up and went over to the window. Somehow, I knew she'd be there, and she was, standing beneath the window. She wore cutoffs that ballooned around her thin, stark white legs. Her top was old-fashioned, sleeveless and with a bold blue-and-green print, and her hair was pulled back in a ponytail. Even from the window, I could tell it was tangled again. I felt frustrated with her suddenly—couldn't she try to be more normal? She gestured at me excitedly, asking me to come down, and I sighed, feeling resigned, and went to get my shoes.

3.

When I was with my friends in Windsor Terrace, we did regular kind of girl stuff. But being with Tenny was different. We both loved the idea of fairies so much that we pretended we believed in them. We found a huge, gnarled old tree a few blocks from

Abuela's apartment and decided it was a fairy kingdom. The tree sat right by the street, and the sidewalk had buckled around it, exposing some of the roots. When we sat at its base, we didn't see the cars passing by or hear the elevated train on McDonald Avenue. We just saw an ancient kingdom where fairies would want to live. The tree trunk was enormous, the bark thick and dense. We didn't try to peel off chunks of it. We perched on the slabs of defeated concrete and pointed to parts of the roots.

Here is a bridge for the fairies to cross, I can still hear Tenny saying in her strange, scratchy voice. *It's the entrance to the kingdom. Once they cross the bridge, everything belongs to them. See how the roots go up and down? The fairies slumber in these dips and slopes. They sit with their wings aflutter on these knots, these rough gnarls.*

We brought a sketchpad and drew a map of the kingdom. We labeled the bridges and the shelters and the lakes. Tenny was very good at drawing, and she somehow managed to both represent the way things really looked and make them magical too. She had a bin from her old house in Park Slope that was filled with art supplies, simple things like pipe cleaners and glue, but also a wondrous assortment of odds and ends: tiny fabric flowers, bits of gossamer, and cloth remnants that looked like the faded wallpaper you might find in an old, vacant house—once vivid and bright, now long forgotten, the patterns of tiny leaves and buds nearly invisible. We made our own fairies, twisting the pipe cleaner into bodies, cutting dresses from the faded fabric, adding wings and crowns of roses. We made tiny books for the fairies to read. And the fairies had conflicts, drama.

Bow your head, relinquish your crown! Tenny commanded. And then later: *I forgive you. All is forgiven.*

Sometimes we took candy down into the basement of Abuela's apartment building. There was a garage, a laundry room, and a door at the very end of a corridor that had a small sign: FALLOUT SHELTER. The door was never locked and it opened into a tiny room. Tenny and I liked to think we were the only ones who knew about it. It was our secret room. We brought down a blanket and sat on it and ate jellybeans and pretended we were survivors of a nuclear fallout. Tenny described what it would be like, and it scared me a little. Even just pretending we were the last people on earth made me uneasy. Tenny seemed to like the idea, and it did seem safe in a strange way. But I didn't want to be stuck with her forever, with no one else to talk to or play with.

4.

Tenny loved making prank phone calls. We huddled around the phone together—at her apartment if Iris was sleeping, or at mine if my parents were out—hearts pounding. "Hello, I'm calling from the refrigerator repair company," Tenny would say in her distinctive, scratchy voice after dialing some random number. "Is your refrigerator running?" And if the stranger on the other line said *Yes*, Tenny would shriek out "Then you'd better go catch it!" Not everyone took the bait. Some people just hung up, or were confused, or yelled at us to stop wasting their time.

We called Corvi Welliver. Tenny had looked up the Wellivers' number in the phone book, and she brought it over to Windsor Terrace on a piece of her father's old stationery. We both pressed our ears to the receiver as we listened to the phone ring. My heart beat very quickly.

And then, a young male voice. Corvi.

"Hello?"

"Hi," whispered Tenny, trying to disguise her voice. "This is the, um, refrigerator repair company. And we called to ask, if, if, if your refrigerator is running?"

"Let me just take a look," said Corvi, and Tenny and I looked at each other, wide-eyed. "Oh my God, it is," he went on. "Holy shit, it's running away, it's trying to escape! Come back, refrigerator!" He dropped the phone and we heard his footsteps pounding as he pretended to give chase. "Come back here, you fucking *bitch*!" There was a tussle, as if he was wrestling with something. "You piece-of-shit fridge," he hissed, suddenly back on the phone. "You think you can get away from me? You'll never, ever get away from me. I'm going to make you wish you were never *manufactured*." He laughed, his voice low and drawling. "I'm gonna fuck—you —up—"

Tenny slammed down the phone and we stared at each other, breathless.

We called him again after that. Sometimes we just listened for when he said *Hello?* and then hung up, flushed and giggling. But by then, I had a little secret that I held close: I had a crush on Corvi, too, even though I'd only ever caught the most fleeting glimpses of him— striding by us, making spooky noises at Tenny, a Coke in one hand and a cigarette in the other; or sitting above the street on a fire escape with some of his friends, sneakered feet dangling, jeering at the people down below. He was Tenny's crush first, so I pretended to be indifferent. But even the sound of his name made me feel flushed and excited.

Abuela knew who he was. She called him *Rubio* because

of his unusual hair. He became one of the neighborhood characters to speak of or gossip about whenever something bad happened, as if he was solely responsible for every instance of robbery, vandalism, or fire—especially fire, for Corvi was known as a kid who liked to watch things burn. Anything that had been set ablaze—a charred, smoldering shopping cart by the train station or the oozy, blackened remnants of a soda bottle that had been filled with newspapers and then lit on fire—was all assumed to be Corvi's handiwork.

"Where are the *parents?*" my mother would murmur when Rubio came up in conversations. My Dad would call him a *bad seed*. And if I was in earshot, I'd find myself smiling.

5.

Tenny started smoking. If I smelled smoke in the lobby of Abuela's apartment building, I'd know she was waiting for me in the fallout shelter. There were even echoes of cigarette smoke in the house in Windsor Terrace when Tenny was there. Mama was not happy.

"Your friend's been smoking in our house, Analie," she screamed, waving her hands theatrically in front of her face.

"Yell at her, don't yell at me," I screamed back.

"I will, when I see her. She sneaks around," snapped Mama, who was no longer as sympathetic towards Tenny as she'd once been. She felt that the older, teenaged Tenny was trouble.

"How do you even get in here," I would mutter irritably at Tenny when I found her smoking in Abuela's fallout shelter, but I already knew. Tenny liked going into buildings and ringing every buzzer to see if someone would let her in, and then roaming around or going up onto the roof. I did it with her sometimes, but I didn't like the feeling of being so high up, or the way Tenny stared down at the streets below so intently, like she might jump at any moment. Sometimes she brought food, like fruit or sandwiches, and threw the remnants over the low wall so she could watch them go *splat*.

We went to Park Slope, and Tenny showed me the house she'd grown up in.

"That was my window," she said wistfully, pointing to the second floor of the looming, stately brownstone. Then she tugged on my arm. "Look, see those paper clips?"

I wasn't sure what she meant at first, but then I saw a little chain of metal paper clips dangling from one of the window bars. "I made that," she said. "I put the clips together and hung them from the window before we moved. So that I could pass by and always see them."

"Why?" I asked, even though I thought I understood.

"It's like—it's like my past life, waving at me," she said, and waved back.

6.

One weekend when she climbed through my bedroom uninvited, Tenny said she needed my help with a plan. We sat on the bed with the phone between us, and Tenny told me what to do. Tenny was fifteen, and I was thirteen.

My hands were sweaty as I dialed Corvi's number, which I now knew by heart. I kept one finger on the cradle so that I could hang up in an instant if necessary.

"Hello?"

"Hi," I said, my voice quavering a little. "Is this Corvi?"

"Yeah. Who's this?" Corvi already sounded amused, as if he knew what was happening.

"You don't know me," I swallowed, hard. "But I know someone who likes you."

"Oh, yeah? Who?"

"She's your—your secret admirer. She wants you to guess."

"No shit," said Corvi. There was a rustling sound. "Hold on a sec, lemme take off my jacket. I just got in. Okay, I'm ready."

Tenny's eyes were bright, and the brown spot around her iris, in her right eye, almost seemed to pulsate. She was biting her lip, her cheeks flushed, and her face was infused with color. She looked like a different person.

After some rustling, Corvi spoke again.

"So do I know this secret admirer?"

"Kinda," I said, looking at Tenny, who nodded at me.

"Did we go to school together?"

"No."

"Are *you* my secret admirer?"

"No!" I was smiling, starting to feel relaxed. Corvi's voice, and the sound of him breathing on the other end of the line, made me feel strangely close to him. I wished Tenny wasn't there.

I heard the popping of a can, and then a series of gulps as he drank.

"Whoo," he said finally. "Oh, man. God, I needed a cold one."

"A cold what?"

"Beer, dummy," he said, and Tenny and I gaped at each other. "Okay. So my secret admirer didn't go to my school. Gotta be a Gravesend thing. Does she work at the supermarket?"

"No..."

"Does she live on my block?"

"Yeah."

"She does! Okay." Corvi took another swallow of his cold one. "Oh, wait. Wait a sec. Hold on. You're not talking about —you're not talking about the dead girl, are you? The one with the drunk mom?"

I forced myself to look at Tenny. The color was disappearing from her face like water down a drain. Now she looked even whiter than usual.

"I don't know who that is," I said quickly.

"Oh, thank Christ," said Corvi. "I don't need that kind of secret admirer. We call her the dead girl because she looks like a corpse, like someone pulled her out of the Bay. I heard her place is a total shit hole and that her dad is dead but they keep his mummified body at the table so it's like he's there with them—"

I hung up. Tenny and I stared at each other again.

"What a jerk, Tenny," I said consolingly. "He sucks, anyway."

I felt bad for her, I really did, but there was also a part of me that was glad he didn't like her. This way, I could pretend he belonged to me.

7.

As I got older, I spent more and more with my friends in Windsor Terrace, and I didn't invite Tenny to join us. The one time I tried to have everyone together at my birthday party, it was a disaster. All the girls wore jeans, but Tenny showed up in an old blue dress that had white lace at the collar and sleeves, looking more than ever like a discarded doll. She spent the entire time sitting sullenly in our living room, refusing to talk with anyone—unless I had to walk past her. Then she grabbed at my arm, calling my name in her cracked, raspy voice, trying to rope me into listening to a story or doing something that excluded everyone else. Every now and then I heard murmurs from the other girls of *Is she okay?* and *What's wrong with her?* She'd had a growth spurt, and her white limbs stretched out like some kind of insect unfolding itself in slow motion. Her presence was oppressive, an imposition. When it was time to have cake, and everyone sang to me, Tenny's voice was the loudest. But she didn't sing the normal birthday song. "Hippo birdies, two ewes," she sang out in her scratchy voice. "Hippo birdies, two ewes." I smiled tightly at her, trying to telegraph that she could stop. *I get the joke but now you can stop.* But she wouldn't stop. I glanced at my mother's face and saw her own curdled smile as we tried to drown Tenny out.

I decided not to invite her to any more birthday parties.

8.

During my senior year of high school, at Mama's urging, I sometimes did schoolwork at Abuela's during the week.

Abuela was getting old, Mama said, and she needed company. Once in a while, when I let myself into her lobby, I could smell Tenny's cigarette smoke. Her cigarette smoke was distinct from anyone else's, with hints of mold and baby powder. Tenny was going to art school in Manhattan by then. When she visited Iris in Gravesend, she always tried to see me, too, never calling first, just popping up—falling into step with me on the street, or climbing through my bedroom window, or even just being close by and hoping that the scent of her cigarette smoke would announce her and bring me to her. But sometimes I pretended not to notice the smell and went directly upstairs. When I did force myself to detour, to push open the heavy door of the fallout shelter, Tenny would be sitting there smoking, eating candy, and leafing through a magazine. I'd say, "Hey," and she'd respond with her usual "Hi, Leelee," a hopeful look on her face that immediately blanched into sadness when she saw my expression. Sadness and something else—a rueful kind of acknowledgment, as though I were just confirming some-thing she already knew, which was that I was hardly ever happy to see her.

"I gotta go upstairs—" I would say, gesturing towards the ceiling, and Tenny would murmur in that scratchy voice that it was fine, totally fine, she just liked sitting in the shelter, she didn't need me to be there.

But sometimes when she showed up in my bedroom in Windsor Terrace at night, I welcomed her. Nighttime was when I was the most frightened about life, when I needed company the most, and that was when I felt the most warmly towards Tenny.

Tenny called these nighttime feelings "the scaries." She

had said when we were kids that the scaries were afraid of light, and that's why they only came out when the sun went down.

She told me stories to help me get sleepy.

The scaries versus the fairies.

During the day, the fairies lounged on the slopes and crevices of their kingdom, and the weather was always sunny, even when it rained, Tenny would say, her raspy voice cracking. *Nighttime is coming, nighttime is coming. The fairies start scrambling off of the roots, trying to find cover. They know it's going to be time soon—time for the scaries to come out, time to hide.*

Tenny told me that 3AM was statistically proven to be the most dangerous time—the time when studies showed that terrible things happened. The only way you could escape the bad things was if you were asleep. I tried to fall asleep so that I wouldn't be awake when the clock turned to 3AM. If I was still awake, I kept my eyes tightly shut. Open eyes made me vulnerable. I believed it. Even in high school, I believed it. Or maybe I didn't believe it, but I felt it. My old baby doll, perched on a shelf directly opposite my bed, was a combination guardian angel and bad luck charm—I wasn't sure which. I thought she might keep the scaries away. But in some way, I blamed her for the thing that had happened to me. If I hadn't been holding the baby doll at the family party, maybe Uncle Gene never would have noticed me. He wouldn't have had anything to joke about, any questions to ask. When I imagined it going this way, I saw myself without a doll, being presented to the grownups, and this time I held on tight to my Dad's hand and Gene didn't say anything. My inner voice, retelling myself the story, was a scream: *Don't let go of Dad's hand! If you don't let go, Gene won't—he won't.*

He won't.

But he always did.

Tenny and her stories helped me fall asleep. She whispered to me about the fairies and the scaries, and there was something about it that made me feel like we were two ghosts caught in a moment of the past, with no bad feelings between us or anything to argue about. No one could hurt us any more. It wasn't just Tenny who was the Dead Girl, it was me, too.

II.
Grown-Ups

After I dropped out of my first year of college—or flunked out, or both—I worked as a full-time nanny to a little boy in the south Slope named Brook Barrett. I had a story I told people, like Brook's parents, that I would be going back to school imminently after having had a personal problem. A family crisis. A hiccup. Sometimes I even told that story to myself. But I had no intention of ever going back to school. Even the thought exhausted me.

Reese and Mia Barrett both worked full-time in Manhattan. Mostly they left me to my own devices, but sometimes Reese got an idea in his head about something we should do, and he made us do it. I could tell it made him feel fatherly.

"Brook loves cats," said Reese one day, and instructed me to take Brook to a puppet show that was all about cats. I spent more time with Brook than Reese and Mia did, and I wasn't sure that Brook loved cats, but I dutifully hauled the stroller and giant diaper bag to a musty little puppet theater

27

about a twenty minute walk away. I wanted to just sit and rest while Brook watched the show, but as soon as the cat puppets made an appearance, he began to scream and I had to get up and haul us out again. We ended up going to a playground. So much for loving cats.

"*¿Como estás?*" Reese asked flippantly when I walked through the door, bumping the stroller in. He was as white as they come, and had the worse accent I'd ever heard, but he liked to throw some Spanish around to show how *simpático* he was.

"*Bien,*" I said automatically. I turned the stroller around and unbuckled Brook so Reese could scoop him out of the stroller and throw him in the air over and over. Brook's squeals sounded a little joyful but mostly terrified.

Inwardly, I shook my head.

"How was the puppet show, kiddo?" Reese was ostensibly asking Brook, but I answered. That was how we did it. Reese and Mia asked Brook questions, and I answered for him.

"It was great," I said flatly.

"Good, good," said Reese smugly. "Did you like the cats? *Meow, meow?*" Brook stared at him. "How do you say *cat* in Spanish, Analie?"

"*El gato,*" I said. I folded up the stroller and folded my arms over my chest.

"We'd love for Brook to be bilingual," Mia had said to me when she and Reese had interviewed me for the job. *Why don't you let him learn English first,* I had thought, but I didn't say that. As it was, none of us had ever heard Brook speak a single word. Not even baby gibberish. Screaming and crying, sometimes, or that blank stare.

Reese thanked me for taking Brook to the puppet show

and said I could go home early. I didn't argue about it, I just gave Brook a kiss goodbye. He stretched his arms toward me and his face crumpled, but Reese held him tightly and mouthed, *Go*. So I left.

I walked. After almost an hour, I was back in Gravesend, thinking idly about food for lunch, and certain that I could smell saltwater, the ocean air making its way down Avenue U from Coney Island. I breathed in, trying to capture that unique scent, salt and sand and the subway. I thought about Reese Barrett, how clean he always looked, and his clothes—collared shirts, sweater vests. I thought about Mia, who so often seemed like a whisper next to Reese's heartiness. She had red hair down to her waist and very pale skin that was covered with freckles.

I felt a hand on my shoulder.

"Hi, Leelee."

I flinched and turned around.

"Did I scare you?" Tenny smiled at me tentatively and then her expression turned wounded. Or pretend-wounded. I thought I saw a little twinkle of malice in her eyes—like she was happy she had scared me. "I'm sorry, Leelee."

I groaned and kept walking.

I had given up pretending to be Tenny's friend or being glad to see her. I was never glad to see her anymore. I wanted to make her go away and leave me alone forever, but I couldn't seem to get the traction, the foothold to really get rid of her. Every interaction was like slipping and floundering. She never gave up. Even just walking beside me, she moved quickly so she could stay by my side, and she was too close. It was oppressive, like standing in front of an open oven.

"Shouldn't you be in art school?" I said it contemptuously, and then regretted it, because it revealed how jealous I was of her life, going to art school on a scholarship and living in Manhattan with roommates. She still called and stopped by unannounced, and even sent postcards, even though we were only separated by the East River. I knew she also came to Gravesend visit her mother.

"I have the day off," she said distantly. "I thought we could hang out. Sit by the fairy tree, maybe."

I started to make an excuse and then changed tactics.

"Tenny, I have to go home. I have a whole life of my own. We're grown-ups now. I can't just go—hang out by the fairy tree."

"Oh, *hubby* wants you home?" Her tone was scornful. "He doesn't want us to be friends?"

Despite everything, I felt a little thrill when she said the word *hubby*. It reminded me that I was married. I had moved on, I had won the prize. Being married was an accomplishment, it was what Tenny and I had always daydreamed about. She had art school and a scholarship and the city, but I had love. I had a husband.

"It's not him, it's me," I protested. "I—I need you to stop showing up all the time, following me like this. It makes me —I feel like I'm on edge, like I'm gonna jump out of my skin." The back of my neck was prickling. What was I so afraid of? She wasn't going to hurt me. But why was it so hard to make her leave me alone? "People grow apart, Tenny. It happens. We had a lot of fun when we were little, didn't we? Oh, God," I moaned when I saw the tears welling in her eyes. "What are you crying about?"

"Leelee, I miss you," she said tremulously. "I miss our friendship."

"Make other friends. Please. Aren't there people at school you like?"

"I don't want other friends, I just want you, Leelee! You were the only friend I ever had—what happened? Why did you do this?"

"I didn't do anything," I said, and I could feel it—something wet and sour rising in my throat.

"Why did you do this?" she repeated. There were a few people on the street, here and there, starting to look over at us. and I began walking quickly with my head down. *Please don't let me get sick on the street, please don't let me get sick on the street.* But even just thinking about it sped up the process, and the next thing I knew, I was at the curb bent over, clutching my stomach, a river of black fluid streaming out of my mouth and into the street.

"Please go away, Tenny, please," I said in between retches.

I heard her sigh heavily and she retreated, whispering goodbye.

I gagged a few more times, and sat on the edge of the curb, waiting to see if it was really over.

"You okay, Miss?" A male voice. Kindly.

"Fine. Sick." I kept my eyes closed and didn't look up.

"She's fine, I got her. *Ay, bendito.*" It was another voice, this one female and accented a lot like my Abuela's. I felt a presence kneeling beside me, putting a hand on my back. "I was walking by and saw you throwing up," she went on. "I know about getting sick on the street, let me tell you. I got shrimp at a place in Bensonhurst with my ex-husband. We was walking home and I said *You know what, I don't feel so good*, and then the next second I was throwing up just like you, only that son of a bitch, you know what he did? He distanced himself from me. He was afraid of germs. He held himself back—wouldn't help me up, wouldn't walk with me. I had to go home all alone covered with vomit. And you know what? I never ate seafood after that. Well, I'll eat fish, but nothing with a shell. I got you, I got you." I allowed myself to focus on this surprisingly soothing monologue as she helped me up, and finally opened my eyes. "You know me, right? Camila. Everybody knows me around here. What's your name? Annabelle, right?"

"Analie." I recognized her from the neighborhood. She was older and had an oval face, small eyes outlined in with eyeliner and mascara, and black hair pulled back severely and twisted into a bun.

"I knew your *abuela*, God bless her, is she still in Florida?" Camila linked her arm securely through mine. "I'll walk you home, don't worry," she said. "Are your parents in Florida too with Isabelle? God bless them. What a terrible thing. I don't blame them for moving. I woulda done the same thing, that happened to me." She went on talking and I half-listened, desperate to get home. "Is your husband at home?"

"I'm not sure," I whispered. "He works in the city, his hours are funny. He's—"

"He's NYPD," Camila said knowingly. "Everyone around here knows that. He's really made something outta himself. You know how boys are when they're young, they're so wild. My son was always gettin' into trouble before he went into the army, now he's got a wife and kids, although his ex-wife, she's somethin' else..."

She knew where we lived and led me home. To my surprise, instead of leaving me at the entrance to the building, she waited with me while I unlocked the door and insisted on taking the elevator upstairs with me. "I'm gonna walk you right into your place, make sure you're okay," she said. "God forbid you fall down in the elevator, hit your head..."

Camila banged on the door before I even had a chance to use my keys, and Corvi opened it almost immediately. He was home, after all. I felt my legs go weak, I was so relieved. He put his arms around me and I leaned against him.

"What the fuck happened?"

"She's okay," clucked Camila. "Maybe she ate something bad. She threw up in the street."

I felt Corvi's hands on my shoulders, and then he was looking into my eyes, his jaw clenched. I started to cry.

"Did you see Tenny? Did she say something to you?" I lowered my head. "I knew it," Corvi snapped. "This is bullshit, Analie. I'll go out right now and find that bitch, I'll settle this."

"Don't, please!" I cried out.

"Don't do anything rash," urged Camila, getting right into the drama. The two of them helped me over the sofa, where I sank down and curled up, pulling my knees against my chest and listening to them talk. Behind my closed eyes, shapes and images swam this way and that like aquatic fish, with their dialogue as a backdrop.

"Corby Welliver," I heard her say to him, almost admiringly. "Look at you, all grown up. I heard you're NYPD now."

"It's Corvi," he said dryly, but he sounded amused. "Corvee. Short for Corvus."

"Oh, that's real nice, it's different. Is it French?"

"No, it was my mother on acid when she named me," he said. I heard the crinkle of a carton of cigarettes and the flick of his lighter. "You want something?"

"You got ice water? I could feel a headache coming on, I know that means I need to drink something."

"Can I get you a drink that's a little more interesting?"

Camila laughed. "It's early..."

"It's happy hour somewhere," I heard Corvi say charmingly, and then the sound of glasses being clinked around, the refrigerator door opening and closing, Camila murmuring some vague, insincere protests about her blood sugar. Then Corvi came over to where I was lying down. I kept my eyes shut. "She's sleeping," he said with a sigh. "Did you see what happened?"

"No, I was walking down the street minding my own business, and when I turned the corner, she was at the curb, throwing up her guts right into the street. She's changed, you know that, Corvi? I been seeing her all around the neighborhood since she was little, I was friendly with her grandmother. She's a pretty girl, but she's been looking sick for a long time. No meat on her bones. This could be stress, she could be sick from stress, with her whole family moved to Florida."

"I'm her family," said Corvi with an edge in his voice, and I felt my stomach tighten with anxiety.

"Yeah, you're all the family she's got now," said Camila soothingly. "But something's wrong. You take her to the doctor?"

Corvi was silent for a moment, and when he spoke his voice was softer.

"It's not that," he said.

"What is it, then? Maybe I could help you."

"I don't see how." Corvi's voice was weary. "This fucking bitch won't leave her alone. They have a history. And she just can't move on. She will not move on."

"I know," said Camila. "I know who she is."

"So then you know that my hands are a bit fucking tied, here," said Corvi. "I'm a cop, I should be able to handle this, but I don't know what to do."

"I know someone," said Camila. "He's my landlord. He can help. You know him too, you seen him around. He's got a pretty little wife and two kids, one of them's almost grown up. *El cuandero*. The witch doctor…"

III.
Fire In The Hole

1.

During my first semester at Brooklyn College, I met a guy. His name was Cameron, Cam for short, and he was a senior. He was my height, compactly built, with deep-set eyes and a thatch of dark hair, and a beard he wore neatly clipped. It tickled my nose when we kissed. He smelled like aftershave and mint mouthwash. His East Village apartment was immaculate, too, from the perfectly arranged stack of books —all about movies and filmmaking—on his coffee table to the record player, neatly covered, on a shelf by the windowsill. On one wall there were two clocks, each with a different time ("One is New York, the other is Paris time," he told me carelessly. "My ex-girlfriend was French.") Outside, a tree drooped against the fire escape, leaves rustling. And in the bathroom, he had a photo taped up, a man and woman facing each other in profile, foreheads almost touching. The woman wore a striped shirt and had very short, cropped hair. The man was cupping her face in his hands.

I still lived in Windsor Terrace with my parents. Mama thought it was ridiculous for me to live anywhere but home, given that my school was in the very same borough. "I'd live at home too, if I had your mom to cook for me," Tenny said, reassuringly, when I told her that I'd be commuting to Brooklyn College.

Everything about Cam's life was unusual and exciting to me—the five flights of stairs up to his apartment, the bathtub that sat in the middle of the kitchen, the way he was always doing things like going to lectures, or concerts in Central Park. Everything about him was something I could become, and all of it held me in its thrall. But after two weeks, he stopped calling. Soon after, I saw him on campus with his arm around a girl who had vivid red hair and wore a silky green jacket, reminding me of a praying mantis with its head chopped off.

The death of that hope—of imagining myself as a part of everything that made Cam's life special—made me feel sick with disappointment. I left school, even though I still had classes that day, and I walked for miles instead. I found my way to a luncheonette with a phone booth in the back. The operator's voice, when I called to get his number, sounded disapproving, like she knew I was pursuing someone who didn't want me.

I wasn't sure if he'd even be home yet, but bile was in my throat as the phone was ringing.

"Hello?"

"Cam?" My voice was tremulous.

"Who's this?"

"It's—it's Analie."

"Ah, Analie," Cam said. He lowered his voice. "I've been thinking about you."

I started to cry.

"What happened?" I finally choked out.

He chuckled. "What happened? The cat was away and the mouse did play. And playing with you was so lovely, Miss Analie. You're amazing. I'm still thinking about you and the things we did here."

"I saw you today, on campus," I said, and I heard him sigh. "Was that—do you have— a girlfriend?"

"Yes," he said, pointedly regretful and still speaking in low tones. "She's a very nice girl, and I should treat her better. She's *sure*, you know? She's completely sure about us, but I'm just—I'm *not* sure. And I don't know exactly where the root of my ambivalence lays." He sighed again. "I need to get my act together. You and I can always be friends, Analie, and I promise if anything changes between Maureen and I, well, you'll be the first to know. I think you're such a cool person. You know that. We had fun, didn't we?"

"Her name is Maureen?"

"Oh, Analie," said Cam, exasperated, and I hung up the phone. It was the only thing I could do—hang up without saying anything else. My head was bowed. It was not the head of a princess. I would never preside over the tiny kingdom of that East Village apartment. I felt sick, and I wanted to crawl outside of my skin. The train ride home was blurry through my haze of tears.

I itched, too. Between my legs, it itched so much that it hurt.

2.

The itching had been with me for a little while. There had been so many sensations after being with Cam—the aching where he'd been inside me, the tingling on the skin of my neck where he'd buried his face and scratched me with his beard—that I hadn't paid attention to the itching. All that had gone away, but the itching got worse. It had developed from a muffled kind of prickling in my pubic hair to a nipping, maddening, biting feeling.

When I got home, I told Mama I was sick. She made me sit down at the dinner table anyway with her and Dad and have a few miserable bites of food.

"I hope you feel better by tomorrow, Analie," said Mama. Was it my imagination that her expression was knowing, disapproving? "We're going to your Abuela's. And then in two nights, your Uncle Gene is coming over."

"What?" I looked up from my plate and my head swiveled between Mama and Dad.

Dad didn't look at me, but Mama still had that maybe-disapproving expression.

"We're going to your Abuela's tomorrow night and then the night after that, your Uncle Gene and Aunt Carole are coming over," said Mama impatiently. "Your dad hasn't seen his brother in a long time, I'm gonna make a nice family dinner. So, I need you here. No galivanting around." She smiled slightly then, but she definitely meant business.

"Tomorrow night is just Abuela, but she wants to see you. She got some dresses for you on sale and wants you to try them on."

The last little bite of food I had was suddenly sticking in my throat and I was afraid it wasn't going to go down. I grabbed my glass of water and took a sip, but I couldn't make that go down either and it sputtered out past my lips.

"Analie, are you all right?" Dad looked at me, concerned.

"I'm sick," I whispered. I got up and went upstairs and Mama called after me with questions that I ignored. In my room, I stripped off my jeans and socks and got into bed wearing just a shirt and panties. Mama burst in without knocking just a minute later.

"What's the matter with you, Analie?"

"I just feel sick, Mama," I said. "It's not a big deal."

"Do you want something? Water, or tea?"

"No, I just wanna rest."

I waited until she left and then I slipped my hand down into my panties and scratched. I scratched at myself until I finally fell asleep with my hand between my thighs.

I woke up so late at night, it was almost morning. The sky outside was the vivid blue of an anticipated sunrise. The itching had woken me up, and I began to claw and scrape again.

I scratched and scratched and scratched. I could feel skin collecting beneath my fingernails, and then I felt something else. I pinched my finger and thumb together and squeezed, and then brought my hand up so that it was silhouetted against the window.

Outside, there was blue sky with the shape of a tree

41

against it in black, like a paper-cutting. And between my fingers, like a movie monster in miniature, was what appeared to be a bug of some sort, plump from feasting on my blood, its legs wiggling. I let out a strangled cry and crushed it between my fingers, then flailed around for the lamp beside my bed. When I turned it on, the baby doll on the shelf was illuminated and I stared at it for a long, agonizing moment. I knew the scaries had won. They always won.

Of course Uncle Gene was coming back. It had been amazing, really, that I hadn't seen him for so long. For years I had worried about hearing those dreaded words—*Uncle Gene is coming to visit*—but no one had ever said it, and I'd relaxed. That was part of the problem, too. I'd let down my guard. I was so stupid for having thought I could be a normal girl and live a normal life. Whatever the bad luck charm, I had brandished it. Whatever the superstition, I had broken it. Was it Cam? I had let him put his hands on me, I allowed him inside of me, I gave myself in to how good it felt, and this is what happened. *I am so stupid*, I thought. *I will never be clean, never be normal. Not ever.* I pulled down my underwear and stared down at myself and saw nothing, as if the fat bug had been a nightmare, but when I batted at my pubic hair I could feel tiny little lumps. I was trying to scrape them away with my fingernails as I stumbled into the bathroom in just a t-shirt, locking the door behind me.

I looked around wildly and grabbed a shaving razor from its resting place on the window sill and began to shave at the hair between my legs, catching flesh in the process and feeling that strange, seamless unzipping sound the skin makes when it's cut with something very sharp. *Ziiip. Ziiip.*

Could I really hear it, or was I just feeling it—that opening of flesh? It hurt, but that was okay. It felt right. I kept slashing at myself until the insides of my thighs were wet with blood. Looking down presented a nightmarish contrast—I hadn't seen myself hairless since pre-puberty, but the blood welling up from where I'd cut myself made it look like I'd lost my virginity to some kind of monster. And maybe I had.

I didn't mind the pain because it felt so much better than the itching. And it was punishment not just for the parasites but for me too. Stupid. Dirty. It didn't hurt enough, so I cut more. I had a hard time holding onto the razor, everything was slippery, and finally I sank down to the floor, breathing heavily, clutching at myself. I felt opened and exposed. Shredded. I didn't want to see what I had done. Instead, I grabbed for a towel and held it between my legs without looking down, and hoped I had made at least some of the bugs go away.

I sat there for a few long minutes, listening to myself alternating between breathing and whimpering. When I finally lowered my gaze, blood was seeping through the towel. I suddenly touched at my long black hair, still held back in some semblance of a ponytail. Had I felt something on my scalp? Something pinchy or itchy? I staggered to my feet, letting the towel fall to the floor. At the bathroom sink I pulled a pair of nail scissors from the medicine cabinet and began to cut off my hair. I gripped at chunks of it, holding it taut, and used the scissors the same way I'd used the razor. I sawed and sawed away. The floor was covered with my hair —the little tiny pieces like spidery confetti, and the big fat curls that looked like the kind parents put in photo albums over the words *Baby's First Haircut*.

Then I cleaned up.

A calm had settled over me. It was a relief. I got down on my hands and knees and gathered all the hair with toilet paper until I had used up the roll, and stuffed it all into the bathroom wastebasket. I cleaned the blood that had pooled on the floor, and I found sly specks of it in corners and behind things.

The sun had come up by then.

I showered—just rinsed, really, to get rid of all the tiny hairs—with lukewarm water, and had to keep from crying out when the water streamed between my legs. Then I got dressed. Gingerly, I pulled on a clean pair of panties. I put on a loose pair of jeans and a giant old sweater I'd bought at a thrift store. Mama was always pestering me to throw it away. I used my hands to smooth at the hair on my head, which was short and fringy with some longer parts sticking out here and there. It took some digging but I found an old gray hat and pulled it on. Then I made my way downstairs as quietly as possibly. When I opened the front door, I heard my mother's voice from upstairs.

"Analie, where are you going? Are you all right?"

"Yes, Mama," I called out. The sound of my own voice startled me. I couldn't remember the last time I'd spoken out loud. On the phone with Cam, maybe, the day before? "I'm going to class."

"You're not sick anymore?" She didn't wait for an answer. "Don't forget we're going over to your Abuela's tonight, and Uncle Gene is coming with his family tomorrow for dinner," yelled my mother, still upstairs. She was always yelling at me from far-away places in the house. I hated it. I hated the sound of her voice when it was loud like that. And she was always repeating herself. She'd be saying it over and over again, as much as she could: *We're going to Abuela's tonight, and Uncle Gene is coming with his family tomorrow for dinner.* She would never get tired of saying it.

"Okay," I yelled back. "Bye."

She started to say something else, but I closed the door firmly behind me to make the point that I was leaving, and I hurried towards the subway as quickly as I could. I got off at Avenue X and found a pharmacy.

"The instructions are inside," said the pharmacist flatly, peering at me from behind oval glasses as he handed me a box. "And don't forget to wash everything. Make the water as hot as you can."

My head, which had been hanging low, jerked up when he said this. "Oh, yeah," he went on, his tone almost smug. "Wash every single piece of fabric you've touched since whenever you picked up this—problem. Otherwise, they'll just keep popping up. On you, on anyone you live with. They're determined little buggers, that's for sure."

Suddenly, I saw myself over the past couple of weeks. I was snuggling under the covers in my parents' bedroom, because they had a TV in there. I was stretched out on the couch downstairs, surreptitiously scratching at what was then a mild, manageable itching. I was drying myself off with a towel that I carelessly tossed back on a hook in the bathroom for everyone else in the house to use. And all the while, the bugs were multiplying. They were spreading everywhere.

I asked to use the bathroom at a restaurant down the street and jammed myself into the stall to use the solution I had bought at the pharmacy, sharp and stinging against the torn, sensitive skin. I didn't recognize myself down there, it was one stripe of hot, raw, crusted flesh crisscrossed with another, and another, and another, all of it trying desperately to scab over, fighting against an overlay of ooze—and losing. A fiery pink color radiated from between my legs to the insides of my thighs and creeped up towards my belly button. There was a little plastic comb in the box, but there wasn't any hair left to use it on.

I was pulling up my jeans when I remembered that one of my finals was taking place at that exact moment.

I stared at my watch, trying to will it not to be true, wondering for just a moment if this was all a nightmare, and then knowing it wasn't.

There was nothing I could do. The exam was happening, and I couldn't make it to school in time even if I wanted to.

I couldn't make it. And it was an automatic failure.

I went to Coney Island instead.

3.

My hands were jammed in my pockets as I walked on the sand, staring at the ocean. Underneath my jeans, I throbbed with pain. I could feel my underwear adhering to my torn skin, glued with blood and smarting from the solution I had just splashed onto myself.

I kept turning it all around in my head, over and over.

Why had I brought the baby doll to the family party that day? Why couldn't I have left it at home? I tried to calm myself by reimagining it again. *No doll. Don't let go of my father's hand.*

My failed class. I had never failed a class—or an exam, or

even a quiz—in my entire life. As far as my parents were concerned, the only excuse for failing a test was to be in the hospital or dead. The same went for missing school. In high school, I had won the award for perfect attendance.

There were monsters on every side of me. If I had to admit to missing a final exam, it couldn't be in a house that was crawling with bugs. It just couldn't be. My parents would find out. They would get the bugs. And now they would never, ever believe me about Gene, because I was a stupid dirty girl who had sex with someone I hardly knew and became infected with bugs. They might think I deserved to be with Gene. Maybe he was coming for me, and this was the component that would help him broker the deal. *She's dirty anyway.* The situation was impossible.

The expanse of ocean in front of me seemed to simplify it all, as inviting as bathwater. All I had to do was walk in until my feet couldn't touch the bottom and then give myself up to the tide. I didn't know how to swim. I would drown. The idea was not just tempting—it seemed like an inevitability, the only feasible solution to my problems. I couldn't take the exam, and I couldn't kill all the bugs. I couldn't run away because I had nothing of my own and didn't know how to live without my family. I had no money, and I didn't know how to do anything. I'd never even changed a light bulb.

Then the sun was slipping down behind the horizon. Where had the hours gone? The water looked dark and cold, not like bathwater at all. The spray from the crashing waves had left me dripping wet. The beach was gray and depressing. I could see a broken glass bottle, its shards sticking straight up, half-buried in the sand and just waiting for someone to step on it, surrounded by cigarette butts and other garbage—the thick, cloudy slug of a used condom, soda cans squeezed into demented hourglass shapes. Behind me was the mocking, looming structure of the Wonder Wheel. This was where I belonged, not in Cam's immaculate apartment in the East Village with his books and records and the two clocks.

I didn't want to go into the ocean anymore. There were other ways to go about killing myself if I really wanted to—a million other ways. Jump in front of an oncoming train. Take all the pills in my parents' medicine cabinet, although that would entail going home, which I didn't want to do. Jump off a building? Abuela lived in a building. I didn't have my key, but I knew how to get in without it, thanks to Tenny—all I had to do was buzz everyone in the building and see who was lazy enough to let me in without asking who was there. For just a moment, I thought about being on the roof with Tenny so many years ago, eating tuna sandwiches and staring at Gravesend from so high up. All the things she made go *splat*. All those times thinking that that in one split-second, I could choose death if I wanted. In just one leap. So easy. *Splat*.

I trudged back to the subway station and got on the train bound for Gravesend.

4.

It was dark when I got off at McDonald Avenue. The playground beneath the elevated tracks was awash in the yellow of the streetlights, and I could see movement. Two guys were sitting on top of the jungle gym, and another was using the frame of the swing set for chin-ups. One of them had pale hair, the ends glowing in the artificial light. It had been years since I'd seen him, but I was certain it was Corvi Welliver.

My heart was pounding as I drifted slowly toward the entrance to the playground, walking past the bocce courts and towards the play equipment.

"Hey, there's some chick over there," I heard one of them whisper, and then another called out in a sarcastic, pretend-friendly voice: "Hello, can we help you with something?"

The one with the light-colored hair squinted at me and then nimbly hopped off the jungle gym. It really was Corvi. His face was still boyish but had leaned out. His hair was cut short, and he had on a denim jacket and a plaid flannel shirt over a white tee, untucked over blue jeans, and ratty white sneakers.

"I know you," he said, smiling.

"Hi," I said. I bundled my hands into my sweater sleeves and swallowed, hard.

"Join us," he said. "Can I get you a beer?"

"Okay," I said.

"Introduce us to your friend, Corvi," drawled one of the guys in an exaggerated Southern accent as he climbed off the jungle gym. He opened a black bag that was lying on the ground and began to unpack it. His skin was light brown, and he had a headful of tight curls. The third guy, at the swings, never missed a beat with his chin-ups.

Corvi used his keys to open a bottle of beer, which he passed to me. I took a long swallow. I hated the taste of beer, but I took a good swallow, and then another.

"I don't know your name," said Corvi.

"Analie," I said.

"Corvi." He gestured at the other two guys. "That's Ricky, he's visiting for the week," he said, pointing to the one with the curly hair. "Like it actually says *Ricky* on his birth certificate. That's how they do things down South."

"Fuck you, man," said Ricky, and I realized that the Southern accent wasn't a put-on. It was real. "What kind of name is Corvi, anyway?"

Corvi put a hand over his heart and smiled angelically.

"I was named after a constellation," he said, batting his eyes. "Who were you named after, the family dog that fucked your mom?"

I let out an unexpected snort of laughter, and then looked quickly over at Ricky, to see how he would react. He shook his head, intent on what he was doing, and muttered "Go fuck yourself, asshole."

"And that's Timmy Falcone," said Corvi, gesturing to the guy at the swing set. "What's up?" said Timmy, breathing hard. He was wearing sweatpants and, even though it was chilly, a sleeveless white shirt. Corvi finished off his beer and threw the bottle against the squat brick building that housed the restrooms. There was the tinkling sound of breaking glass, and I thought of little kids arriving at the playground the next day. At least the weather had turned chilly and they'd have shoes on. Corvi smoothly took out a pack of cigarettes and squinted at me again. "You get a haircut?"

I put a hand up to my head, to my hat, and I touched at the tufts of hair that stuck out.

"I went to the beach," I said, although that didn't answer his question.

"It's colder'n shit today, what the hell?" said Ricky, looking up at me skeptically.

"Smoke?" offered Corvi, and I said *Sure.* He put two cigarettes in his mouth, lit them and then handed one over to
me. I'd never smoked before and I puffed at it uncertainly. I
drew a tiny cloud into my mouth and then released it. Corvi
watched me with a smile that was almost tender.

"I saw your friend today," he said, arching an eyebrow.
"The dead girl."

"You mean Tenny?" I'd been surprised that he remembered me; now I realized that he was connecting me with
her. I wondered if he knew, or suspected, about the phone
calls all those years ago. I hadn't seen Tenny in a few months,
but I'd gotten her postcards with hand-drawn fairies and
messages like *I miss you, Leelee* and *Call or write me, please!*

Corvi shrugged.

"I guess." He shrugged. "Now *that's* a weird name."

"It's short for Tenacity."

"No shit," remarked Timmy, who had walked over to us.
Corvi handed him a beer.

"Where'd you see her?" I asked, taking another swallow. I
must have made a face involuntarily, because Corvi smiled
again.

"Just walking up the block, maybe goin' to visit her
mom?"

Ricky spoke up. "You guys know a dead chick?"

"Nah. She's this girl from my block, she looks like a
corpse," said Corvi with a mock shudder. "Really spooky, like
the whitest skin you've ever seen, and she's got freaky eyes.
We used to call her the dead girl."

"Nice," said Timmy, and Corvi shrugged.

"Uh, Corvi? Could we stop with the smokin' now?" It was
Ricky. "Unless y'all wanna blow us sky high?"

Corvi grinned and flicked his cigarette off toward the bocce courts. "Let the lady finish," he said grandly. "And then we can proceed."

"Thank the Lord," muttered Ricky. "I thought you was pussyin' out on us."

"What?" Corvi leaned forward and smacked Ricky on the head, hard. Ricky let out a yelp. "I never pussy out, man. I'm always *in*."

Ricky said "Okay, okay!" and rubbed at his head. "I didn't mean anything by it. Just thought you were fixin' to follow the law from now on."

"I ain't gonna follow the law," snickered Corvi. "I *am* the law."

I glanced between them again, and then over at Timmy Falcone, who was leaning against the monkey bars.

"Corvi's NYPD," he said, and when my mouth dropped open, he elaborated as though I was stupid. "He graduated from the police academy and started on the job a couple months back."

Corvi was watching my reaction, and he laughed again.

"Don't you know you can be anything you want to be?" His expression turned serious. "I was only ever caught once for all the shit I pulled. And my record got expunged, 'cause I was a juvenile. All I had to do was keep my nose clean since then—or at least, not get caught with a dirty nose. I should definitely not be doing *this*. But Ricky rolled into town so... might as well make it a send-off." He crouched down beside Ricky. "So whatta we got here?"

"A goddamn arsenal," drawled Ricky. "I got two bricks. Smoke bombs. And then a little house-made *spec-i-al-ity* of mine that I call black rockets. We gonna send you out in style, son."

"I can't wait," said Corvi, and he rubbed his hands together, then looked at me. "Are you in?"

5.

Corvi and Timmy Falcone and I all watched as Ricky kneeled over a thick square of something wrapped in plastic and bearing a yellow label that said SUN CROW SUPER CHARGED BOMB CRACKERS. A black bird was silhouetted against an orange sun, and beneath it in smaller letters were the words WARNING - EXPLOSIVE and some very small print. Ricky slit the package open with a pocketknife. They looked like little cigars tied together.

"You need a match, man?" breathed Corvi.

Ricky shook his head, taking out a lighter, and then said "Shit, I almost forgot." He reached into the pocket of his jeans and took out his wallet, thumbed through it, and removed a small plastic bag. Inside it were pills. White ones. "Anyone?"

"Ricky makes it, we call it M&M," Corvi whispered to me helpfully. To Ricky he said, "Can't, man. I'm going back on the job this morning, can't start out on any kind of trip."

"Timmy?"

"No, thanks."

"Bottoms up," said Ricky cheerfully, and he placed one of the pills onto his tongue. He dry-swallowed it, rubbing at the skin of his throat. Then he held the bag out to me. "Help yourself, Miss Analie."

I looked at Corvi and he said mildly, "Try it. I ain't going anywhere."

Imitating Ricky, I put the pill on my tongue and then looked questioningly at Corvi, who nodded. I swallowed it down with some beer.

The guys took turns lighting the firecrackers and throwing them into the adjoining ballfield, where they crackled and sparkled and sounded like rapid gunfire, tiny bullets. *Like fairies shooting guns*, I thought. In the houses that surrounded us, lights began to come on, and someone shouted at us from a window.

"Light one, Analie," said Corvi, and he handed me a firecracker and a lighter. I fumbled with it at first, then stared at it once it was lit. "Throw it, throw it!" he yelled, and I did.

Pop pop pop pop pop.

"Let's move," said Ricky, gathering up his little bag. "My car's just down the street."

"Hold on," said Corvi. He was rustling through Ricky's black bag. He pulled out a brownish lump with a drooping wick sticking out of it. It looked like raw cookie dough. Corvi lit it and threw it in the direction of whoever had shouted at us from the building that was closest to where we were standing in the playground. It landed on a fire escape with a clatter, and an angry face appeared in the window.

"Step back, motherfucker," said Ricky, and we watched a thick stream of smoke pour upwards from a dancing flame, which then became a plume of fire. All three men around me screamed with triumph, and I did too.

"All right, let's go," Corvi was laughing, and we broke into a run, following Ricky's lead until we reached a beat-up, rusted maroon Buick.

"I'm taking off," said Timmy Falcone, and he kept jogging, down the street beneath the elevated tracks, rounding the corner, and into darkness. "Don't kill your-selves out there," he called behind him. Wordlessly, Ricky passed his keys over to Corvi, who unlocked the rear door so Ricky could climb into the backseat, then gallantly opened the passenger door for me and crossed around to the driver's seat. "Gimme the bag," said Corvi, and Ricky's hand appeared from behind us, proffering the black bag, which looked almost like a doctor's kit. I glanced at Corvi, who started up the car and stuck an unlit cigarette behind his ear. The radio blared on at the same time.

"Let's drive," he said.

I buckled myself in and Corvi smiled in profile, looking over his shoulder as he pulled out.

And then suddenly my head snapped back.

I took a deep, harsh breath of air.

My eyes were wide open.

My mouth was wide open.

I was drinking in a new world.

Oh, my God.

"Something's happening," I whispered.

"Easy, it's the M&M," said Corvi. "Just relax, baby, go with it."

There was an echo, in a whisper.

Easy, it's the M&M. Just relax, baby, go with it.

EasyitstheM&Mjustrelaxbabygowithit.

I reached for him, grabbing at his arm, startled at the way the fabric of his coat pulsed beneath my fingertips. I could feel every thread, and the warmth of his skin beneath.

"I can't move," I mumbled, and Corvi leaned over and

unbuckled my seatbelt. I felt better as soon as it loosened. The light changed and Corvi stepped on the gas, one hand bracing my shoulder so I wouldn't fly forward through the windshield. Then he put his arm around my shoulder and pulled me close. I found his hand and maneuvered it against my face, breathing in the smell of burning, and then I brought two of his fingers into my mouth. I heard his sharp intake of breath.

Then he chuckled. "I need that hand for a minute, to drive."

Ineedthathandforaminutetodrive.

INEEDTHATHANDFORAMINUTETODRIVE.

Mouth now empty, I tried to bring my teeth together, but I couldn't. My jaw seemed to lock each time I tried. I needed something, like a horse's bit.

"Lollipop," said Corvi, and Ricky said from the backseat, "Yes, please."

"I'm not offering you a lollipop, asshole, I'm *asking* you for one. For *her*."

"Glove compartment. Fetch me one too, will you?"

Corvi seemed determined to keep driving, but he swerved a little as he reached over me. Finally, he screeched to a halt at a stoplight and popped open the glove compartment. A mess of junk—receipts, papers, wrappers, an empty Coke bottle, and a crumbling mess of Ritz crackers—was released, all of it expanding slightly and then falling to the floor. "Christ," said Corvi. He rifled around and finally pulled out a fat purple ball of a lollipop, unwrapped and exposed and dotted with crumbs and other bits of detritus. I slowly rolled my head toward him and watched as he sucked it clean, spat out the window, and then handed it to me.

When I didn't respond, he stuck it in my mouth and my lips obediently closed, pursing together.

I moaned at the sheer force of the sugar. Grape flavor. Lollipop, picked straight off the vine. The candy vine. Surely there were candy vines in the fairy kingdom. Tenny would like that idea. She loved candy. The fairies' little feet padding across the thick roots, lifting in the air for the moments it took to pluck the candy off the vine. It was almost too much, I had to take little sucks and swallows. Corvi glanced over at me with a smile on his face.

"Where's my lollipop?" asked Ricky in a faraway voice, and Corvi said, "I found one and gave it to the lady. You'd give a lifeboat to the women and children first, right?"

"Are we sinking?" I asked urgently, and he said "No, no, baby. It was just an analogy. I meant we'll keep you safe, no matter what."

I needed to focus on those words. Fortunately, I could read them as they passed in front of me, one by one.

WE'LL

KEEP YOU

SAFE

NO MATTER WHAT

"You mean from people who want to hurt me?" I needed to make sure. "Keep me safe from anyone?"

Corvi looked over at me again, his brow furrowed.

"No one's gonna hurt you," he said. "I'm not gonna let that happen." Then he felt around in the black bag and pulled out another of the doughy-looking lumps, which he threw into the backseat. "Open your window a little more, dude," he called over his shoulder. "I don't trust your aim." Wind filled the car. I gripped the seat and laughed, closing my eyes, giving myself up to the rollercoaster of air. I was positive that even over the roar of the wind I heard the flick of Ricky's lighter, because I could hear and feel everything now. The lighter over the wind and the night noises. The texture of the seats beneath my fingertips. Ricky yelling, "Fire in the hole!" and the two men whooping with victory as we left a small explosion in our wake. They did it a couple more times, a few blocks apart. Each time, when I twisted around in my seat, it looked like we were being ejected out of a cloud of cotton candy.

"It's beautiful," I murmured.

"This ought to keep 'em busy for a spell," remarked Ricky. "Meanwhile we can find us a bigger fish to fry."

"What are you talking about?" The words tumbled out of me like I was throwing up alphabet soup.

"Important rule of firefighting, Miss Analie," said Ricky. "Never pass by one fire on your way to put out another. If the firefighters around here are any good, they're gonna stop and put out these little campfires before they start chasing us. My father is a fireman," he added.

Corvi laughed, and I said, "You're kidding."

"Oh, I'm as serious as smoke inhalation," said Ricky. "I grew up in a small town, for sure, but my daddy taught me everything I know about how to set a successful fire. The old man had no idea what he was doing. Thought he was giving me lessons in fire safety."

"Meanwhile, he's like 'Yeah, Dad, sure,'" mimicked Corvi breathlessly, and jerked his hand up and down, fingers touching. "'Tell me more, Dad.'" Ricky howled with laughter.

"Ever seen a car on fire?" Corvi asked, and I shook my head. He made a harsh turn and when I slid along the seat and against him, he put his arm around me again and kept one hand on the wheel. I looked out the window as we whizzed through a very industrial part of Brooklyn. It was like we'd traveled back in time before people moved here and built their cozy little homes—or had we traveled forward, when everyone had left?

The lights of Manhattan glittered across the choppy river. The bridges connecting the boroughs were magnificent. We left them behind and were soon surrounded by four-story walk-ups on tree-lined streets. As the walkups turned into brownstones, the foliage seemed to grow more plentiful, more lush.

"Well, now, I see this is where the high-class folk live," Ricky remarked, leaning forward.

"Yeah, well, fuck them," said Corvi. "Here comes the burning class. Ricky, you on lookout?"

"Already ahead of you, man. Just don't go so dang fast. I can't see anything."

I wondered what Ricky was looking for, but I didn't feel like formulating the question. Instead, I explored Corvi's arm around me, marveling again at the feeling of his skin underneath the layers of fabric. How terribly sad that we didn't have this kind of sensory ability on an everyday basis —we were missing out on so much. I reached the bare skin of his wrist, the tiny hairs, the knob of his wrist bone, and then finally his hand. I put his palm against my mouth and breathed in a lifetime of him: smoke and burning, of course, but also cigarettes, and beneath that soap, and the clean flesh smell of someone who's just been born. It was so warm, so sumptuous, that I let out a little moan. Corvi laughed and shifted in his seat.

Suddenly, Ricky was leaning over from the back seat again, propping his chin on his hands. "We just passed one, brother." With his shock of curly hair and his excited smile, he looked like a little kid at an amusement park. "Back it up."

Corvi obligingly put the car in reverse, slowly, and Ricky said, "There."

I looked curiously out the window at a row of parked, undistinguished cars.

"You see it?" asked Corvi, jerking his chin forward, and I shook my head no. "The window's open."

I focused on the dark green Plymouth to our left. Sure enough, the rear window had been left open a couple of inches. Both Ricky and Corvi opened their doors, almost in unison, and climbed out of the car, circling the Plymouth. Corvi felt around in his pocket and pulled out a coin, which he flipped in the air and then smacked down on the back of one hand, concealing it with the other. "Call it," he said, and Ricky squinted, in deep thought. "Come on, man. Just call it!"

"Heads. No, tails."

Corvi rolled his eyes and then revealed the coin. "Tails. Enjoy. You are a guest of this great city, after all."

"Why, thank you, sir."

I got out, too, and peered into the back seat of the Plymouth. Two car seats, some scattered toys. I looked around and tried to get my bearings. It seemed like we were in Park Slope—very close to Windsor Terrace.

Corvi appeared by my side with a red gallon container.

"Let's get you back in the car," he murmured. "I want you safe and sound." I did as I was told, settling back into the front seat. Corvi reached in and turned on the ignition, then winked at me. "We'll be ready to roll in just a minute," he said. "Don't touch anything, though."

I heard a muffled, grating crunch of glass—Ricky had broken the Plymouth's rear window with something wrapped in what looked like a greasy towel, which he then used to poke at some of the remaining shards so that they fell to the ground. Glancing around quickly, Corvi carefully tipped the container up against the broken window, fluid gushing from the spout directly into the car as Ricky stood back, hands in his pockets, watching. Corvi spoke to me over his shoulder in a low, instructional voice.

"You want to set a car on fire from the interior," he said. "I mean, sure, you can douse the exterior and then light it, but starting on the inside is much more satisfying and it actually does the most damage." He returned the container to the trunk of the car and closed it firmly but as quietly as possible. Then he got into the driver's seat next to me and inched the car forward a few feet. "Fire in the hole," whispered Corvi. I craned my neck to look past him at Ricky, who was lighting a match and then, seemingly in slow motion, tossing it through the opening in the Plymouth's window. There was a split second of suspended time, and then an enormous ball of light and a sound like the entire city clapping its hands once. Then Ricky was climbing into the back seat and hissing, "Go, go, go!"

Corvi took off, and I twisted around in my seat, desperate to see the car burn. I saw the ball of light flatten and seep over on the sides like a thick, molten liquid. I was desperate to see more, and I realized we were circling around the block, maneuvering so we would pass by again, this time on the other side. He slowed down so we could appreciate the full spectacle. The Plymouth poured fire at every angle. You could turn it upside down and it would have made as much sense—the black and orange billows poured from the roof, but then at the bottom, it flowed in big gushes from the wheels, too. Even though the flames were so vividly colored, they were topped with the blackest smoke I'd ever seen.

Lights were coming on in the houses around us, just as they had when we set the firecrackers off in the playground, and people were yelling and screaming. There was a loud, sharp popping sound, and then another. Right before our eyes, the hood of the Plymouth seemed to shudder, and then it flew up with incredible force and smashed violently into the windshield, breaking the glass, releasing more fire, thick and unyielding, pure fury. Finally, Corvi peeled out. He had only driven a few minutes before he eased into a parking spot and turned off the ignition. He scrunched down in his seat and I did the same, snuggling into the crook of his arm. He squeezed me tightly, and we waited, hearing pops and crackles from blocks away as the car continued to burn, and then sirens in the distance, coming closer, and then firetrucks screaming by us, one after the other. I screamed too, as ecstatic as if I were on the Cyclone, and Corvi laughed out loud, holding me close. When there was a break in the stream of emergency vehicles, he pulled out and we drove along at a normal speed, almost serenely.

"My eyebrows are gone," said Ricky from the backseat. "Singed clear off."

"You're still marvelous, darling," said Corvi, and the two men began laughing again.

Minutes passed. I wasn't sure where we were headed, but then I got the sense that Corvi was just driving aimlessly, one arm still around me, still chuckling to himself and singing along softly to the radio.

"Can we go to Windsor Terrace?" I heard myself say it as if it came from someone else—like there was another girl sitting beside us in the front seat, and if I turned my head even a little, I'd see her giving me a sidelong glance with a smile on her face. I wanted to talk to her and ask her what she meant, but it would have been for show. I knew exactly what she wanted to do.

"Sure," said Corvi. "Tell me where to go."

I sat up straighter, figuring out where we were, getting oriented as I became aware of Greenwood Cemetery whizzing by on one side of us. I directed Corvi down a side street, then another, and then my house was coming into view and I said, "Right here."

We all sat there, thoughtfully contemplating the little two-story structure with its blue-gray exterior. There was a strip of grass in the front. The yard was in the back. All the lights were off upstairs, but the living room glowed orange. They always left that light on, and the house was so incredibly still that I knew they weren't there. I pictured Mama and Dad at Abuela's. They were probably all awake, wringing their hands, wondering where I was. At that moment, the phone inside the house began to ring. There was a pit in my stomach that was making me feel sick, like I was about to throw up. I imagined myself doing my home-work at the kitchen table while Mama bustled around. Now the house crawled with bugs that we could never get rid of, and a monster was on his way. Why had I forgotten to be afraid of him, why had I thought he'd just disappear? Of course he was back. Monsters came back. This was the only way.

"I'm sorry," I whispered.

But it was barely even a whisper. I was mouthing the words.

Ricky's voice piped up from the back seat.

"If a volcano erupted next to the ocean, who do you think would win, the lava or the water?"

"What do you mean 'if?'" Corvi's voice was scornful. "That shit happens all the time. Lava's always falling into the ocean. It turns to stone, you fucking jackass."

"I'm just thinkin' out loud, man. Jee-zus H. What are we even doing here? Whose house is this?"

"Lava and ocean," snapped Corvi. "They're living in sin."

I laughed and listened to the sound of my own laugh. And it *was* my laugh, there was no other girl in the front seat with me, it was my laugh and my smile and it was me who pulled Ricky's black bag off the floor and into my lap.

When I opened it up, at first I thought it was empty.

"Where is everything?"

Then I realized I was looking at a half a dozen black objects that were barely visible in the dark of the car and against the black fabric of the bag. I took one out and I heard Ricky's intake of breath and his voice, soft:

"You'll wanna be careful with that."

"What is it?"

"My black rockets," he said. "I made them specially back home and brought 'em up with me."

I examined the one in my hand. Like the firecrackers, it also resembled a cigar, but it was wrapped in black paper. Two things were sticking out of one end: a long, thin wooden stick, and a twisty piece of black string. I held it to my face and breathed in, getting a whiff of what I could swear was the kind of glue we used in school, and then something unfamiliar.

"How does it work?"

Ricky cleared his throat. "Uh, well, you'll wanna stick the wooden part there into something to hold it steady—"

"Like dirt?"

"Sure, like dirt. And that there black piece is the fuse."

"What's inside?"

"Well, uh, I make my own rocket fuel." He paused, uncertain if he should go on. "Uh, so for that, well, I use potassium nitrate, of course. I got two kinds of charcoal in there—one is for the spark trail—and an itty-bitty amount of sulfur. That's all. The black paper is just tissue paper. I call it a black rocket, it should be black."

"I want to light them," I said.

"You can light them," said Corvi kindly. "Just not in the car. Show us where, so we can help."

I led them up the front walk. The path became a bridge behind me. When we were done there, I'd walk across it one last time—and then I'd be in a new kingdom. Everything would be different.

New ruler.

New rules.

I held the moon and the sun between my thumb and my

index finger and brought them down to the size of baby teeth that I rattled in my palm like dice.

We stood on the doorstep at the front door in a jumble, as if waiting to be let in. The street was utterly quiet. Every house on the block had its eyes closed. But Ricky didn't like it, I could tell. He raised a finger to his lips and jerked his head, and we followed him around to the side of the house. There were two windows, and both of them were cracked open. Beyond them was the warm, glowing interior of the empty house. Below them were window boxes filled with the heartiest fall perennials my mother could find.

"You sure 'bout this?" Ricky asked.

"They're in Gravesend," I said, nodding.

"Naw, what I mean is—y'all sure you want to do this?"

"I'm sure," I said.

"You heard the lady," Corvi murmured, and he carefully handed me the black rocket.

"Welliver, I think you found your soul mate," Ricky said with a heavy sigh. "God love you crazy kids."

I felt my mouth curve into a smile when I heard the words *soul mate*. Gingerly, I aimed the long wooden stick into the soil of the window box and pushed it down into the dirt so that it leaned towards the interior of the house. The window was open. Only the screen separated the rocket from the living room.

"Excuse me," said Ricky politely, and he leaned over me and sliced at the screen with a Swiss army knife that he'd pulled out of his jacket pocket. The rocket was now pointed directly into the house with nothing to get in its way. Corvi hoisted up the black bag, and we all reached into it without another word. When we were finished, there were three black rockets at each window, pointing into the darkness. Ricky fussed over them, pulling at the fuses slightly so that they curled up a little.

"Just so you know—" Ricky began, and Corvi stopped him.

"She knows," he said.

Ricky shrugged. "Okay. You hell-bent on lighting 'em yourself? I wouldn't if I were you." He rolled his eyes and made a face when I stayed silent. "You gotta be steady as all hell, do one after the other, and then back away real fast and get in the car, you got that?" I nodded. "All right, wait till I start 'er up."

"I'll stay here," said Corvi, and he smiled at me. He passed me a lighter.

"Thanks," I said. I tested it out, feeling every single ridge of the spark wheel on the flesh of my thumb. I heard Ricky start the car and I hit the red button. A flame wobbled to life.

"Fire in the hole," murmured Corvi.

I leaned forward and with perfect precision, began to light the three rockets at the first window. One. Two. Three. They started to hiss and smoke. My fingers were burning. I darted over to the second window and did it all again.

Four.

"—Go, go, go," Corvi was whispering —

Five.

"Come on, guys," called out Ricky from the car, his voice cracking in a hoarse whisper.

Six.

Corvi grabbed my hand and pulled me away, jerking me around the house and down the steps. Across the bridge. New ruler, new rules. We made it to the backseat of the car, just yanking the door closed as the first rocket went off with a sizzling, crackling *whoomph*. Ricky pulled out, tires giving a short squeal as the other rockets went off with that same noise: the hissing, and then explosive release. I looked out the window as we drove away, and I saw the windows of the house lighting up like the flaming, pageful eyes of a jack-o-lantern. The door was the mouth, and it roared at us. Corvi was watching with me, and I heard him gasp.

"It's gonna go up," said Corvi with awe in his voice.

Ricky slowed down as we reached the corner and we all turned around to watch. The street was still utterly silent except for a kind of wordless bellowing, a thundering and a cracking. I heard shattering glass and watched the end of the block light up. The light flickered but never dwindled; instead, it got brighter and brighter.

"I bet close up it's even more beautiful," whispered Ricky.

"Yeah," said Corvi admiringly. "Come on, we gotta get out of here."

"Where to?" Ricky asked, and Corvi looked at me.

"The cemetery," I said, pointing. "It's the other way—okay, keep going—down East 5th—now make a right."

We flew down Greenwood Avenue, passing my block again, which was now bathed in orange. People were running down the street in bathrobes and pajamas, shouting. "Down Greenwood," I said. We reached MacDonald Avenue, and the border of the cemetery in just a few short blocks.

Corvi reached into the front seat and slapped Ricky on the shoulder. "Maybe you should keep going, man," he said. They exchanged a fist bump.

"You got it. I'll be back in *Ju*-ly," said Ricky. "Peace, brother. Pleasure, Miss Analie." I could hear fire trucks in the distance, and Corvi gave Ricky one more slap on the shoulder and then climbed out of the car, pulling me with him.

"Bye, Ricky," I called out, but he was already screeching away.

"Over the gate?" Corvi said, gesturing to the cemetery, and I nodded. "You first." He lifted me easily, waiting until I got a grip on the sharp iron posts. He held me steady and I jumped over, landing with a thump on the perfectly mani-cured lawn, and he followed. He took me by the wrist, and we ran.

6.

We found refuge deep inside the cemetery, at the side of a mausoleum with block letters that spelled out FARIES. At first, I thought it said *Fairies* and I let out a happy gasp, but I looked closer and the letters, as if they had been teasing me, settled into place with the extra I no longer in evidence.

We sank to the ground, and I settled into Corvi's lap, shivering.

He held me tightly, our faces close.

"That was your house," he said.

I nodded.

"It's gone now, are you okay with that?"

I nodded again, and then he was kissing me. His upper lip was glazed with perspiration, and he tasted like salt. I was ravenous for him. Our tongues came together, and I wrapped my arms around his neck, pressing against him as hard as I could. I wanted to swallow him whole. We rolled around like that, our faces smashed together, my head lolling into a bed of moss as I stared up at the treetops and at the sky, which was grudgingly lit with a scattering of stars. When I was on top, I could see blades of grass behind the pink tips of Corvi's ears. I clutched at him with everything I had as we finally came to a stop against a lone, skinny tree some feet away from the mausoleum. The tree shook, and leaves drifted down on top of us as we panted in unison, our chests heaving against each other. "Please, please, baby," he whispered. I didn't know what he meant. But all he wanted to do was hold me. So I held him too, and we listened to our breathing and the sounds of fire engines and ambulances, a truck or a bus screeching to a stop somewhere in the distance, and the nervous chatter of city animals at night. His body pressed against mine elicited both a sharp jolt of pain from between my legs, and a long, aching note of pleasure, as though someone were holding their finger down on a single key of a keyboard.

My hat had come off, and Corvi held my face between his warm hands, staring at me closely. "Your head is like a baby bird's," he whispered, and we kissed. Then he spoke again. "I lied to you before, but I promise I'll never do it again." He was still breathing hard and kissing me between words. "I said I didn't know your name, but I did, Analie."

"How?"

"I used to see you around," he murmured. "You were the most beautiful girl I'd ever seen in my life. I asked people and I found out your name was Analie and you lived with your parents in Windsor Terrace. I couldn't believe it when you walked into the playground tonight... last night... whenever it was...."

"Why did you say that you didn't know my name?"

"I was trying to play it cool," he whispered, and I laughed. Corvi Welliver, playing it cool—for me? He sat up, maneuvering our bodies until I was on his lap straddling him and he was holding me tightly and leaning against a headstone that was right beside the tree. He cradled my head and kissed my face. "Only paper I ever wrote in school was about Edgar Allen Poe, you know him?" I nodded and he went on. "There was this poem he wrote and it always made me think of you—the name of it reminded me of your name. Annabel Lee."

"What's the poem about?" I whispered.

"Two people in love. This guy, and a girl he's known since they were kids." I looked up at him to see if he was joking, or making it up, but his expression was very serious. "The angels are jealous of how much they love each other. The wind comes out, chilling and killing Annabel Lee. Are you cold? I don't want you to get chilled and killed."

"A little. And then what happened?"

"Something like... the angels in heaven and the demons under the sea can't take away Annabel Lee. I think the guy like, sleeps next to her tomb."

"The stuff you gave me is wearing off," I told him.

"Did you like it?"

I nodded, but I felt sad as those limitless thoughts and feelings—that special awareness, the words marched before my eyes as if on the way to face the firing squad, the razor-sharp focus—drained out of me slowly. I silently said goodbye.

Corvi released me just for a moment so he could wriggle out of his jacket. He wrapped it around me and leaned up against the headstone again, pulling me back into his arms. I curled up against him, my head on his chest, his warm hands on my sore scalp. Some more firetrucks screamed by, followed by another ambulance. Their lights washed the cemetery with red.

"Can we go by the house and see it?" I asked.

"Hmmm," he said thoughtfully. He was speaking more slowly, as if he were falling asleep. "Generally, you're not supposed to revisit the scene of a crime... but being that it's your house and all, it would probably be more suspicious if you stayed away... Where was your family?" I told him they were in Gravesend at my Abuela's. "Okay, sure," said Corvi. "Let's—let's stay here a minute and then we'll go back, okay?" He held me tightly. I still felt sad. The fabric of Corvi's jacket had ceased being magical. The grass around us, lit by the yellowish glow of nearby streetlights, no longer sparkled as though I were holding a match to every blade. I hoped I could hold on to what I had learned—that there was a whole other world out there where you could feel what you'd never been able to feel before and know the sound a flame makes when it first ignites, and rule everything with fire. Corvi would be my link to that world.

I didn't know I was falling asleep, but the intimate blue of the late night sky was suddenly gone. Now it was a flat white, lit with a bashful—and totally unimpressive—golden blush by a sun I couldn't yet see. Corvi whispered to me, saying we should go. Otherwise, we didn't speak as we stood up and stretched our stiff limbs. I found my hat and put it on, and we brushed leaves and dead grass from our sleeves, our jeans. Corvi tightened his jacket around my shoulders, protecting me against the chill of the morning, and we walked quietly and cautiously to the gate that bordered McDonald Avenue. Cars were whizzing by, but there were no pedestrians. We left the way we had entered and walked side by side back to what was left of my family's house.

7.

It was unrecognizable, and it reminded me of a variety of physical grievances. The raw cavities of missing teeth. A ribcage blown apart by a spray of bullets. What else? The family dog, run over by a car. Someone's face, beaten to a pulp. The entire structure was still smoking, and lit by the red flashing lights of the fire engines that were parked haphazardly up and down the block. A mix of police officers and firefighters were gathered outside, reflective yellow stripes mingling with the letters NYPD. People stood on the outskirts, still in pajamas or wrapped in blankets. The air around us burned hot but damp, a nauseating medley of smells. Some were familiar, like a fireplace, but others were alien to me—chemicals and burning rubber, the logically stinking smell of a home set ablaze and then soaked with water.

And something else.

Corvi kept his arm around me as we approached, and at that exact moment there was a rustling, a mumbling, and I heard someone say, "They're here." But no one was looking at us—everyone was focused down the block toward Greenwood Avenue. I saw my parents hurrying up the street. My mother was running—she had her hands to her face and was wailing. Dad looked almost embarrassed, as if the crowd around the now-ruined home was a critical one, drawn by something unseemly— incorrectly bagged garbage, maybe, or a broken front walk.

Mama saw me before Dad did, and I watched her take it all in.

Corvi's unusual hair.

Corn silk.

Rubio.

Her eyes narrowed at the sight of his jacket, draped over my shoulders, his protective arm around me. The choppy pieces of hair sticking out from under my hat. Then she looked back at the burned-out husk of our house that still seethed with smoke. Even in the light of the morning, the space behind the windows looked black, and the upstairs was flickering with the white of flashlight beams as the fire-fighters searched the space. It seemed like the houses on either side had been vacated. In particular, the one on the right looked sooty, and two of the windows were broken. My father was standing at the curb, bent over at the waist, his hands on his knees. One of our neighbors was at his side saying, *Easy, easy.*

Then two things happened almost simultaneously.

Mama screamed out, "Analie, what happened?"

Every head in the crowd swiveled towards us.

And a firefighter called out harshly from an upstairs window, my bedroom window. "There's somebody up here!" His voice sounded young, and cracked with panic.

There were gasps. All the heads swiveled back towards the house, and Corvi's arm tightened around me.

At first, I imagined that the person they had found was

me, and that I was a bystander at the scene of my own death. A little of the M&M left, maybe. Or just simple shock. But Corvi's body next to mine felt decidedly real, as did the chill morning air and the dank smell of the burned-out house. There was yelling and commotion coming from what had once been my bedroom. I didn't understand. Who else would be in my room in the middle of the night? Mama and Dad were right in front of me. They had stayed the night in Gravesend. It couldn't be Abuela. Who else—

And then I knew.

I knew.

IV.
So Good To See You

"You're probably gonna feel like shit, coming down off the M&M," Corvi said, tucking me into his bed in the two-bedroom apartment in Gravesend that he shared with his mother. "Try not to think, and just sleep it off. I gotta go to work, baby, I got a court appearance. I wish I could stay." As he spoke, he stroked my face, looking into my eyes. "I'll get you some water. Make sure you stay hydrated, and just rest, okay? Don't do anything. I'll be back tomorrow. And you won't be alone. My mom is here, for what that's worth."

The morning of the fire when he brought me home, his mother Moira came tottering out into the living room to greet us. When she saw me, her eyebrows went up and she smiled and said, "Oh, he*llo*," putting emphasis on the second syllable. She was tall, like Corvi, with bleached blonde hair. She wore a dusky pink bathrobe, and her bony shoulders made the fabric look like it was resting on a hanger.

"Mom, this is Analie," said Corvi flatly. "Analie, this is Moira."

I was practically falling asleep on my feet, and I kept opening and closing my mouth, fascinated by the sound of my jaw clicking. Moira seemed unaware, or unfazed, about it, and about everything else—like our rumpled appearance and that we smelled like smoke and death.

"Hi, honey, I'm so happy to meet you," she said in a voice that was soft at the start but hard at the edges. She took my hand. Hers was bony and cold. "Do you kids want breakfast? I can make you something."

I shook my head and glanced up at Corvi.

"No, thanks," he said in the same flat tone. "Go back to bed."

As if he hadn't spoken, she went on.

"French toast? Pancakes? Eggs, maybe? I think we have some bacon in the freezer..."

"I said no," said Corvi coldly. The pressure of his hand on my shoulder urged me forward. Moira started to say something else, and Corvi interrupted her. "Shut the fuck up, or I swear to God..."

"Okay, Corvi," she said, laughing and giving a little salute. "Let me know if you get hungry. Do you have work today, honey?"

"Yeah," said Corvi. "Listen, Mom. This is important. Anyone asks, we were here all night, with you. Watching TV."

"Got it."

"Take care of Analie for me. Whatever she needs—"

"Of course, and we'll have a great time, Analie! Just us girls!" Moira chirped.

"— but otherwise just fucking leave her alone, you got that?"

Corvi's steered me into his room, which was very small. The narrow bed frame, with its rumpled sheets, looked like it belonged to a kid. A bookshelf was loaded down with textbooks, folders, and papers and he had a dresser with clothes piled on top of it.

Corvi told me he was going to shower and get ready for work, but that I should get undressed if I wanted, and get into bed. I did, and I dozed off, waking to see him standing at the foot of the bed buttoning his shirt, the air around him scented with soap and steam and shaving cream. He tucked me in and said goodbye, and I fell asleep again. When I woke up and realized he was gone, I felt terribly sad. A glass of water sat on his bedside table, touchingly filled to the brim with ice cubes that hadn't yet melted. I slept for the entire day, only waking when Moira poked her head in to ask me if I needed anything. "Any time you want that French toast, just let me know, okay?" Then, thoughtfully, "Although I have to say, I'm not crazy about French toast. I love a good omelet. Do you want an omelet, honey?" I mumbled *No, thank you* and she said "That's fine! I think I'll make myself one, though. And that's the end of the eggs. So if you want something later, it's going to have to be cereal or toast! I need to go do a shop, as soon as Corvi can drive me..." I fell back asleep. In the evening, she roused me, and I went into the dingy, windowless bathroom and was sick to my stomach. "Annie Lee? Are you okay in there?" Moira stood outside the door. "Why don't you take a shower, it'll make you feel better. I can make you some tea. I'll get you a fresh towel..." Moira seemed as starved for company as if she'd been locked in the apartment for years without any human contact other than Corvi. I showered, feeling tears spring to my eyes as the warm water met my torn skin. Gingerly, I pressed my fingers between my legs, against the raw, swollen flesh, wondering if my ability to bear children was in any way affected. I didn't know if I ever wanted to have children. At that moment it was the last thing I could ever imagine wanting. I got dressed again, reluctantly. My underwear was crusty with dried blood.

Moira commented on my shorn hair. She offered me one of her nightgowns, but I said no. It seemed creepy to wear her clothes. I put on one of Corvi's shirts from the pile on top of the dresser and dragged myself back into his bed. When was he coming back? He'd said tomorrow, but I wasn't sure when today ended and tomorrow began. I left the light on in his room. I was afraid to be in the dark. Before, my sleep had been dreamless. Now I was worried that the minute I closed my eyes, I'd be back in front of the ruins of our house. Windows gaping open, stained black at the tops. The flicker of flashlights moving within them. The firefighter's voice.

There's somebody up here!

I wanted to think of Tenny lying there as pristine as Sleeping Beauty, hands folded across her stomach, a slight smile on her lips. I tried to hold on to the image, but it was impossible. I knew she would have been charred black, all her hair burned off.

I did fall asleep, and I did find myself back on the front walk of our house, the window boxes melted and the flowers immolated. I was propelled against my will through the front door and up the stairs towards my room, where she was waiting for me. I was padding down the hallway and I knew her back would be to me, but she would turn slowly when I got to the doorway and I didn't want to see, I didn't want to see—

I gasped as I woke up, so grateful when I realized I wasn't in the burned-out house, but in Corvi's strangely sad little room on his narrow bed. Someone was watching TV in the other room. Moira. I heard the creak of the sofa and her footsteps coming towards me, and I closed my eyes and pretended to be asleep. The door squeaked open, and then she shut it closed with a click and everything went in reverse, her footsteps and the creak of the sofa. I wished Corvi would come back. When was tomorrow?

In the morning Moira made us coffee and toast, and we sat across the table from each other. Her face was fully made up and she lit up a cigarette almost immediately. "I'm so glad Corvi brought you over, even if it was at a very strange hour," she said. "You know he's never brought a girl home before? Oh, he goes on plenty of dates, if you want to call them that. I've always got girls calling the house for him. I think he's a bit of a heartbreaker, if you know what I mean. He says, 'Mom, tell 'em I'm not home.' He does *not* want to settle down. Of course, I'd love to see him pick just one girl. That would make me so happy. But he doesn't care about that. Making me happy, I mean. Annie Lee, I'm going to be honest with you and tell you that I wasn't much of a mother to Corvi when he was a little boy. I suffered from addiction problems. I don't think he's ever forgiven me. He doesn't realize that addiction is an illness just like—well, like having a thyroid problem or chronic back pain. He really holds it against me.

And I do feel sorry for him, he was such a sad little boy. But on the other hand, I'm here for him now. He wants to move out of here as soon as he can, when he starts making a steady paycheck with the police force. But I tell him, I say, 'Corvi, Mommy's here now and she loves you. Why can't we be closer?'" She looked at me expectantly.

"And what does he say...?"

"Oh, he tells me to fuck off," she said. "That's how he talks to me."

"I'm sorry," I said.

I pulled off a soft piece of my toast and ate it, and when I looked up Moira was smiling at me. Her smile was frozen, stretched from ear to ear like it had been carved into her face.

"You eat like a little bird," she said. "You're so pretty and delicate. I love your pixie cut, Annie Lee."

"Tell me about Corvi," I said after a moment. "When he was little."

"His full name is Corvus, did he tell you that? It means a bird, like a raven, but it's also a constellation. I had the most wonderful trip when I was pregnant with him, lying under the stars. He says to me now, 'How could you take drugs when you were pregnant?' But it's a myth, the idea that you shouldn't. The government doesn't want us to have any special insight, we're supposed to lie low and live forever with blinders over our eyes. Of course, they're going to *say* that it's against the law, and dangerous, and punishable by death, and so on. Take it from me—I dropped acid many times while I was pregnant with Corvi and he turned out fine. You see how strong he is. And smart as a whip. He didn't do well in school but it was just 'cause he kept getting into trouble. Typical boy stuff. But the acid had nothing to do with that. And acid was never the problem for me. It was when they started slipping stuff in there, and I know that's why I ended up doing coke. That's the government's solution, to drop poison into all our enlightenment so that we end up killing ourselves only because we're searching for a higher truth. And to tar everyone with the same brush." She shook her head. "God, it feels good to talk about all of this. I try to tell Corvi, but he says to shut up. I want to explain to him, that I was ill though no fault of my own. That's what the bad drugs do, they makes you sick. I went crazy when he was a little kid, I really did. I hurt him. And I let other people hurt him." Tears ran down Moira's cheeks, and she didn't wipe them away. She wanted those tears on her face, for me to see them. They were like a badge of some sort of virtue. "I was seeing someone, too, Analie." Moira lowered her wet eyes. "A woman. You know, the crowd I ran around with, we were very open, you know? And I met Marilyn at a bar in Bay Ridge and she wanted to date me and I thought, why not? Two women together can be a beautiful thing. I didn't know that she was mistreating Corvi. As far as I knew she was helping me, helping us. She used to bring him to day care three days a week and I guess that was no good for him, either. Here I am, finally on the wagon and getting myself clean, going to work, and they're calling me from day care saying the kid won't stop screaming for his mommy. I can't drop everything at this new job and go running off to pick him up, right? So I said, "Tell him I'm coming if you want, if that'll calm him down.' He told me later that they used to lock him up in the supply closet and then let him out a few minutes before Marilyn came to pick him up. I'm sure it disturbed the other kids. And after all that, it turned out Marilyn was no good for him either! She hurt him, Annie Lee. She was out of her mind at the time, drinking and whatnot, but still. I broke it off, eventually. I didn't know what to think at first—kids make stuff up, and he could have been doing that stuff to himself. But I've forgiven her. Corvi won't. Marilyn lives in Queens now—she's scared to death to set foot in Gravesend because Corvi hates her so much. He says he'll kill her the next time he sees her and it doesn't matter what kind of consequences there are. I said, 'Corvi, you might as well kill me, too, then. If not being perfect is a sin, well, then—we're all sinners.'"

Moira smiled at me sadly and lit another cigarette.

"When is he coming home?" I asked.

"Soon, honey," she said. "You're anxious to see him? That's sweet. Sometime today or tonight. I honestly can't remember exactly when. In the meantime, I guess I'll start tidying up..."

"I'll help," I said. I wanted to get away from her. I felt like I was being suffocated with her strangely offhand stories, the decades-old misery of a little boy, and I couldn't stand it anymore. The apartment was neat, but dark and dusty. I opened the windows to let light and air in, and I used a wet cloth to wipe down the tabletops and shelves. I folded the laundry and put Corvi's clothes away, feeling moved at the sight of the very flannel shirt he'd worn the day before. His shorts. All his socks had holes in them. I did the dishes and swept the kitchen floor. The refrigerator's interior was bleak, but I did find some American cheese, and margarine, and there was bread in the freezer. I made grilled cheese sandwiches, very slowly, so that the bread would warm up and thaw and not burn. My father taught me to make the perfect grilled cheese sandwich. He did something unusual, which was to press a clothing iron down on the sandwich while it was cooking, so I asked Moira if she had an iron. She looked at me quizzically but said *Sure, honey,* and she rummaged around in a hall closet and presented me with one. "Look at that," she cooed as I worked. "That's amazing." Soon, I had made three sandwiches, all perfectly flat, golden at the edges and glistening with margarine. Drips of cheese were visible between the crusts. I hoped Corvi would be home soon, because the sandwiches tasted best when they were hot. Moira ate hers, but I couldn't eat. I poured myself a drink of water from the tap in a chipped plastic yellow glass with a faded image of a duck on it. *Corvi's favorite cup from when he was a kid,* Moira told me. I paced back and forth as Moira prattled on and on. I looked out the window, but the apartment faced the back. Then I heard his key in the door and finally, finally, he was standing in front of me, unexpectedly wearing a suit and tie.

His pale hair stood a little bit on end and his eyes were tired, but his face broke into a smile when our eyes met.

"Hi," he said.

I started to say hi back, but Moira disturbed the air around us.

"Corvi, honey. Did you have a good day? We made you a sandwich."

Corvi shot her an aggrieved look and loosened his tie, returning his gaze to me. His lips parted slightly, and we stared at each other.

"I'm gonna change," said Corvi.

"Go with him, Annie Lee, you two get reacquainted," said Moira. "There's a show I want to watch. I'll just be in here—"

I followed Corvi into his room and he shut and locked the door behind us. Still staring at me, he eased out of his suit jacket, revealing a badge clipped to his belt and a holster tucked neatly beside his armpit with an actual gun in it.

"Wow," I said. "You look so—professional."

Corvi smiled. He placed his badge carefully on top of the dresser, followed by the gun and holster. I approached him cautiously, as though he were a cat that might scratch me to ribbons without warning, but he was very still. "Can I help?" I asked, and he nodded. My fingers were shaking as I unbuttoned his shirt. "Do you usually wear a suit? Or a uniform?"

"Depends on the day," he murmured. "Usually my blues but if I got a court appearance..." He lifted a hand to my hair, his face close to mine. "I didn't know if you'd still be here," he whispered, and we kissed.

"Of course I'm here. I've been waiting. I couldn't wait for you to get back."

"Analie," he said against my mouth. "I have to tell you something."

"What is it?"

"The body—the body upstairs—" I kissed him, harder, so that he wouldn't speak, but he pulled back a little bit and said, "You were right. It was your friend."

"Is she dead?"

"Yeah. Your parents were at your grandma's, like you said. They had no idea Tenny was there."

The house had been so unbelievably still. Had I smelled

her cigarette smoke at all? I couldn't remember. Would I have noticed? Would I have cared?

"She used to sneak in, but she hadn't done it in a while," I said. Corvi kissed me again and I spoke against his mouth. "I didn't know, Corvi."

"It's okay," he said, his hands on either side of my face. His breathing was rapid and I could feel him getting hard against me, which made me shiver. At first, I thought he wanted me despite everything, and I was relieved. But then I realized he wanted me *because* of everything, or at least partly. That was even more of a relief, that he knew one of the most terrible things about me and still wanted me. Later, Corvi parted my bare legs and spanned his fingers very, very gently across the hot, slashed flesh between my thighs. Brow furrowed, he looked up at me. "Oh my God, baby," he whispered. "You did a number on yourself, didn't you?" I don't know how he knew, but he did. I nodded and he whispered that all of that was behind us and he was going to take care of me from now on. "You're okay, you're okay," he murmured. "I've got you."

Over the next six weeks I lived in that room and I lived for him and I came to know every inch of him—the jutting of his shoulder blades as he sat on the edge of the bed and shoveled cereal into his mouth before he left for work, the slump to his spine when he walked in after twenty hours in Central Booking. The vestige of old cigarette burns on his arms that he never talked about. The careful way he laid down his badge and gun on the dresser. His stories. Sometimes they made me laugh, sometimes I cringed. His first autopsy. His first dead body, his sixth, his fifteenth. The first time he pulled his gun on someone, the time he got jumped, all the times prostitutes offered to blow him. His shenanigans—a drunken ride in a squad car uptown with his partner Valdez, the time a little kid broke a bottle over his head. Stories about the police academy. "I was worried about passing the psych test," he told me. "Luckily, I had a hook. Like a mentor. He coached me. Once I got the general idea, it was easy. They ask you like fifty different times if you've ever dreamt of running off to join the circus."

"What's the right answer?" I asked

"The right answer is no. They don't want, like, free spirits. They want you to toe the line. And I've never dreamt about running away with the circus. Who dreams about crap like that?" Corvi told me he'd made one mistake: "There's a part on the exam where you have to draw a house. Guy kept telling me, don't forget to put in windows. So I remembered that but forgot to put in a door." So how...? "My hook drew it in for me," he said ruefully.

He was fearless and terrible with his mother and almost funny when he told her to *Shut the fuck up* or said *No one fucking asked you.* His eye-rolls at me when she said anything at all. Comments about her ex-girlfriend, Marilyn were brief: "The two of them, her and Moira, I hope they burn in hell." He was merciless in showing how little he cared for Moira's well-being, emotional and otherwise, whether it was turning on the television at top volume in the middle of the night when he got home late or blasting his radio in the bathroom while he shaved first thing in the morning. He adjusted some of these habits for me, and was touching in the way he tried to be considerate. But since I only lived for him during those six weeks, scarcely knowing the day or time, I was happy to watch movies with him at three o'clock in the morning, make him a grilled cheese sandwich at midnight, and give my body to him any time he wanted. His schedule was mine. He was mine and I was his. I owned his scars and he owned mine.

The police came just once to ask us questions in a bored, perfunctory way, and we gave them our story about hanging out all night in Gravesend, talking and watching movies with Corvi's mother. "Absolutely," said Moira. "They were here all night and so was I." After the police left, she looked at Corvi, beaming expectantly, and he asked her what the fuck she wanted, a goddamn medal? "Oh, Corvi," she said sorrowfully, but he was already headed into the kitchen and slamming things around.

Tenny's funeral came and went. *Do you want to go?* Corvi asked, and I thought of the burned body in the closed casket and my parents and a drunken weeping Iris, and I said *No.* I wanted to feel badly, but I didn't. The times I cried, when Corvi was at work and I buried my face in his pillow and breathed in his scent, I didn't even know what or who I was crying for. But I seemed to have lost my tears. None came no matter how hard I sobbed. I remembered sitting on the beach that day on Coney Island, how'd I'd lost hours and woken up drenched in salt water. Maybe it had been all my tears, instead. Six week's worth, wept preemptively in one afternoon. I didn't even cry when Dad came to see me, Moira standing uncertainly in the doorway of Corvi's room, saying, "There's a man here who *says* he's your father," with a skeptical and paranoid arch of the eyebrow. Of course he was my father, although he looked much older and very stricken and tentative as we stood facing each other in the Welliver's living room. "Do you want to sit down?" I asked and he said no, he preferred to stand. He said this whole thing had about killed my mother.

"She thinks you had something to do with this. Please, Analie. Tell me you didn't. Or go see her and tell her yourself. Please. I—I want to believe that we know you."

I stared at him, my mouth opening, and I could feel the words forming.

No, Dad. I had nothing to do with it. I would never do something like that.

But I didn't say anything. I couldn't. And that told him everything.

Dad cleared his throat, looking almost frightened, and said that he and Mama were receiving insurance money for the house and were taking Abuela to live with them in a condo in Florida. He didn't invite me to come. Instead, he said that I could take over Abuela's apartment, which she owned, as long as I could pay the monthly fees.

"No shit?" said Corvi when I told him the next day. "When can we move?" He wanted to know what Abuela's apartment looked like, and I told him about it—the smell of talcum powder, the old but perfectly maintained furniture. Her tiny refrigerator that hummed, the bed with the iron frame. "Is it king-sized?" he asked. On the nights he was home, we slept together on his bed, which was so narrow that I had to lie directly on top of him. He slept with his arms around me tightly, the whole time, his mouth always open in utter exhaustion.

Corvi brought me things from outside: packs of panties from the discount store down the street, and nail polish. Gum. Pads for when I had my period. He talked about City

Hall and how we would get married there. He bought us wedding rings.

I felt snug within this pact we'd created. And after being in his apartment for almost two months, once I was sure Mama and Dad and Abuela had left for Florida, I stepped outside with Corvi and squinted in the cold, brilliant sunlight. Moira cried when we left. "I'll be here, I'm right down the block. You'll remember your ol' mom, won't you?" she said, touching at the corners of her eyes, and Corvi said, "I'll do everything in my power to forget," while I smiled awkwardly and said, "Thanks for everything, Moira." I carried a single plastic bag filled with my belongings, and Corvi had a duffle. He wore a suit and tie and his badge and his holster underneath, and he carried his uniform, freshly dry-cleaned, on a hanger and slung over his shoulder, wrapped in plastic. The winter had rendered every tree on the block leafless and barren as stone, standing at attention, but bowed, like bystanders at a funeral procession.

As we approached Abuela's building, I saw someone on the corner, watching us.

From a distance, I took in her tangled cloud of hair.

Her old-fashioned print dress.

Her long, white limbs.

I slowed my walk, trying to make my mind work.

Oh, no.

No, please.

It's impossible.

Please.

I tugged on Corvi's arm.

"Corvi," I whispered. "That girl—"

"Hm?" he was lost to the world, seemingly in a reverie, maybe thinking about the big bed we were about to inherit.

"I think—that girl—it's—" I could barely get the words out. "Is that—Tenny?"

"What?" His eyes came to rest on the figure with the tangled hair. I heard him inhale and then a cracked whisper. *"Jesus Christ."*

"Is she alive?" I asked, but then she answered the question for us, glaring with eyes that flashed with fire and then turned to blackened holes as she got closer. Her twisted curls were really smoke. We stood, paralyzed, as she began to move, walking purposefully toward us. Sometimes she was charred and barely human, everything else burned away. Then she became Tenny as we had known her. The dead girl.

She'd always been the dead girl.

After that day, Tenny would know where I was. She'd been able to find me before, but now she didn't even have to look. The needle of her compass, hot enough to sear flesh, would always point towards me. Walking beside her would feel like standing in front of an open oven. I'd see malice flickering in her eyes, the joy she took in ruining my life, to get back at me for everything I had done to her. She would always smell of burning.

The whimpering noises I heard came from me.

I gripped Corvi's arm as at last she stopped in front of us, settling into a bearable visage—Tenny in adolescence. I remembered the dress, the satchel, the childlike angles of her body. I tried to squirm out of this reality as though it were a nightmare and I could wake myself up, but I couldn't. I was irreversibly, inextricably *there*. And so was she. And so was Corvi, who stood beside me frozen in place, his mouth open. She didn't look at him, though. The sockets of her eyes were turned towards me.

Finally, she spoke. Her voice was still raspy like I remembered, but also singed with smoke, painful to listen to and forced out of a diaphragm that was scorched beyond repair.

"Leelee," she breathed, her mouth stretching into a smile. "It's so good to see you."

V.
The Life Cycle

1.

"I know you."

The man was coming down the steps towards us. He was tall and trim in khaki pants and a black shirt, holding two mugs. His voice was warm.

"You do?" I was surprised.

"*Sí, claro*," he said with a smile. "Isabelle's granddaughter —I've been seeing you around Gravesend since you were a baby. Corvi, nice to see you again."

"How're you doing," said Corvi, his arm around me tightly. "Analie, this is the guy—" He hesitated. "This is Mr. Vendeval."

"Please, call me Adán," the man said, directing his gaze back at me. He held the mugs up with a smile and a shrug, showing me that he couldn't shake hands, and we all laughed politely.

"*Mucho gusto*," I mumbled. The sun was behind him, and I put my hand up to shade my eyes. I could make him out, but I couldn't place him, which made me nervous.

"I hope Isabelle and your parents are well." Adán's voice was solicitous, and he didn't seem to mind when I didn't answer. He led us into the storefront entrance just below street level, maneuvering the door open and holding it for us.

The space was cool and quiet. Adán had a wooden desk beside an old checkout counter, all painted white. A potted lavender plant sat on top of a stack of books, and there was a little painting on the wall of a ship being tossed about by dark water. A bunch of plastic bananas were hanging from the ceiling, swathed with cobwebs.

Adán settled himself behind the desk.

"Please," he said, gesturing to the two chairs that sat opposite. "Have a seat."

Corvi pulled my chair out for me before sitting down. Still smiling, with his dark eyes fixed on me, Adán pushed one of the steaming mugs towards me on the table. He took a sip from his own. I could smell coffee, chocolate, and cinnamon. Both men seemed to be waiting for me to drink some of it, so I did.

"So you ran into Camila by happenstance," Adán said. "And your husband has since come to see me. He told me all about your—your former friend, what a nuisance she's become. I'd like to help you."

"How?" My voice sounded weak and wispy. I cleared my throat and drank some more from the mug. Adán took out a carton of cigarettes and held it out to Corvi, who accepted silently.

"A lot of people come to me with their problems," said Adán. He lit a cigarette, inhaled deeply, and then let smoke seep out of his nostrils. "Some of my assistance is practical, and some of it may seem unusual. But the most important thing is that I get results. That's why people come to me. They trust me. And you can trust me, too."

"Okay," I said slowly.

"But we need something from you."

"What is it?"

Time was slowing down and the air in the room seemed thick.

"We need you to bring her here to us, Analie."

I turned to look at Corvi, who shifted uncomfortably in his seat.

"I can't do that," I said. "I don't have any control over her. She does what she wants."

"You have more power than you think, Analie," Adán said. "It's what draws her to you. Can you think of it that way? Like you are a magnet, and she is drawn to you in a way that transcends logic?" I saw his eyes flicker past me, and then there was someone else in the room. I jerked my head around, half-standing up, but it wasn't Tenny. It was a woman with long dark hair, who placed her hand on my shoulder comfortingly.

"I'm sorry I startled you," she murmured. "Please, sit down. I'm just here to help."

"This is my wife, Mariana," said Adán. "*Querida*, did you leave the doors open?"

"Yes."

I turned around again, and the door to the storefront was open.

With all the blinds drawn on the inside of the space, the doorway seemed to glow.

Mariana was speaking to Adán in soft tones. Adán caught my eye and winked.

"Logistics," he said wryly, and shrugged. "They still come into play. Who watches the door and keeps everyone else out? Where are the children?"

"They went to Coney Island," said Mariana.

"All that needs to be taken care of," sighed Adán. "The so-called 'real world' is ever-present. Drink some more."

I did.

Everyone was quiet.

"What do we do now?" I asked.

"Nothing," said Adán. "We wait."

How much time passed? Hours? Could it have been the entire day? The open door still glowed, but in a different shade of light. Corvi held my hand tightly. He and Adán smoked endless cigarettes. Adán drank from his mug. Mariana got up and made the men one cup of coffee after another. Adán said something about a light in the building that kept flickering, and Corvi asked him if he'd tried tightening the bulb. *Or, like, if it's a lamp, try those prongs, you know?* to which Adán replied that the electricity was shit in the whole place. I drowsed in my chair, first feeling embarrassed about it, and then realizing it was exactly what was expected of me.

I think she'll be here soon, Adán said to Corvi. *Do you understand exactly what you're supposed to do?*

Yeah, I got it, said Corvi. *If she'll go along.*

You have to persuade her, Adán replied. *We can't make her do anything she doesn't want to do.*

Their voices receded, and I walked.

I knew that I was asleep, that my body was still, but at the same time, I walked.

I made my way through the land of fairies.

I scrambled over roots, and ducked under the slabs of sidewalk that jutted from the ground and loomed above me.

I sat upon the knots, the rough gnarls. I let my feet skim the little body of water that the recent rain had left behind. I combed through my long hair, using a comb fashioned from a tiny seashell with carefully carved grooves. Now and then my wings of shimmering gossamer twitched as I slumbered amidst the dips and slopes.

I smelled smoke.

Smoke from a fire, smoke from cigarettes, smoke rising off irreparably burnt flesh, and the room was suddenly as hot as I imagined hell to be.

I heard the people around me gasp.

Adán stood up suddenly, knocking over his chair with a clatter. The woman murmured something that sounded like a prayer.

I felt Corvi's fingers entwined with mine. He squeezed my hand tightly, and then let go.

"*What's happening?*" Tenny's voice came out in a roar, her rage ignited. It hurt to listen to—it must have torn her throat apart to scream like that.

I kept my eyes closed, but I guessed there were no mournful eyes, no tentative half smile. Just fire.

"Hey, hey," said Corvi in his reasonable voice, his sweet voice. "We just want to talk to you."

"*Go fuck yourselves.*"

I heard Adán let out an exclamation—something between a laugh and a gasp.

"This isn't a trap," Corvi said. "Come on. Let us explain."

"What did you do to Leelee?"

"She won't have any of it," Corvi's voice had lowered and was seductive. "It has to be between us. He'll help. This is gonna be win-win, I promise."

Tenny simmered. I sensed it.

I finally opened my eyes to see what was going on. Adán stepped in front of me. He snapped his fingers and said, "Go to sleep."

And I did.

2.

"*Mira*, Analie."

Valdez, Corvi's partner, was reaching across the restaurant table, handing me a photograph he'd removed from an envelope marked with the Kodak logo.

I took it, smiling. I'd seen it before in the newspaper, Corvi surrounded by firefighters and NYPD, standing outside of a four-story walkup with a baby in his arms wrapped up in a beach towel. Corvi's face was almost expressionless, with only a hint of a smile. He looked like a child being blindsided by the unexpected flash of a camera. It was the first baby he'd had to deliver on the job.

"I love that," I said. "It's so cute."

"Officer Welliver, man of a thousand gig cards," said Valdez. "Our hero."

Valdez's wife, Stacy took a long sip of beer and told me

how Valdez had almost passed out in the delivery room when she had their first kid. Valdez gave her a dirty look.

"Don't show them the other pictures," called out Corvi from the bar, where he was waiting impatiently for the bartender's attention, and Valdez said, "I ain't gonna" and then to me, "Don't worry, it's not strippers or nothin'. Just dead bodies. Corvi likes to pose next to the real gruesome ones, giving that shit-eating grin and a thumbs-up."

Corvi appeared, toting a fresh pitcher of beer. "I don't know if they really qualify as *bodies* when they've been in the water for the month," he said with a smirk.

"Are you serious?" Stacey shook her head. "You guys are sick."

"I want to see," I said suddenly.

Valdez grinned and went through the envelope, selecting a photograph. Corvi looked over his shoulder critically and shrugged his shoulders.

"Analie's made of strong stuff," Corvi said. "She's not going to freak out."

Valdez handed me the picture.

"You went and got these *developed*?" said Stacey. "You just went into a Kodak?"

"Guy had no idea what the fuck he was seeing," said Corvi.

"If he asked, we woulda told him we found a giant sea anemone in the East River," Valdez added.

Corvi burst out laughing as I leaned over to look. The guys were right. What had once been a human was absolutely unrecognizable, dead white and bloated, looking nibbled and shredded at the edges. And there was Corvi, exactly as Valdez had described him, grinning and giving a thumbs-up. He was in his blues, but hatless, and his hair was plastered to his forehead—whether it was with sweat, or water from the river, I wasn't sure.

"Oh my God, you guys. That's *disgusting*," said Stacey. She shifted away and then smacked Valdez on the arm. "And *you!* You took this picture? I believe *he* would do this"—she jerked her head towards Corvi—"but not you! I feel sick."

"Look at the picture of me with the baby again," said Corvi, lighting a cigarette. "It's all the same thing."

"What the fuck does that mean?" Stacey's voice was shrill, and Valdez winced.

"Cycle of life, honey," Corvi said. "That corpse? He—she, it, whatever—was a baby once, right?"

"Enough, Welliver," said Valdez.

"No, I'm serious. That's how it is, life and death," said Corvi. "One comes in, another goes out."

3.

The phone was ringing. I kept my eyes closed and hoped someone would answer it.I had no idea what day it was, what year, or where I was waking up. I didn't know if it was Corvi's room the day after the fire, or our bedroom, or maybe even my room from when I was a little girl. I had to take stock of every little detail and then put it all together. There was the blanket wrapped around me and the scent of the laundry detergent that Corvi and I used. Very cautiously, I opened my eyes, squinting, not sure what I would find. White and yellow, the colors of our pillows and sheets, the smell of laundry detergent. The light coming into the room was morning light, and decidedly of the present. I felt my entire body give in to a tremendous sense of relief, and I stretched. Corvi was beside me, squirming to get into an upright position amidst the tangle of blankets as he reached for the phone.

"Welliver," he said into the receiver. "Oh, hi...No, it's okay... Really? Has that ever happened before?... Uh-huh... Yeah, it's very strange... I don't blame you at all, man, not at all... This is one crazy city. Okay, let me think for a minute." Corvi rubbed at the bridge of his nose and stifled a yawn. "Oh no, no, that's fine, I was getting up anyway, no, no. Hmmm... Okay, why don't I swing by and we can go to the precinct together... no, your precinct, but at least I can be there to make sure those knuckleheads take you seriously..."

His voice had sweetened, as if he'd stirred sugar and cream into a cup of black coffee. It was something I'd first heard him do the morning after we'd burned my house down, after the firefighter had called down about the body upstairs. Amidst the fresh wave of anguish that rippled through the crowd of police officers, firemen, and onlookers, Corvi tried to pull me away and out of it. We approached my parents —Mama had fallen limply and dramatically to the curb, where she was now sitting with a paramedic. Dad was on her other side, patting her hand, talking to a police officer who was crouched beside him. Then the police officer leaned in closer and asked him something. I tried to walk quickly by them, but Mama saw us and pointed and shrieked, "Analie, there was someone up there!"

Corvi didn't try to get away, he slowed and began speaking with the police officer in a solemn, respectful tone. When I got to know him better, I learned it was something he was very good at—gauging whoever he was talking to and even anyone who might overhear him, and deciding at the very moment which guise to put on, how to speak, what he needed to communicate. It was an ongoing process, trying to grasp what was wanted from him, as tricky as catching minnows with his bare hands. I heard him do it with the police officer, who had a mustache and a badge that read RICCI. First Corvi introduced himself—to my parents' dismay and consternation—and then quietly, humbly added that he too was NYPD—a rookie. The two men shook hands and there was some shop talk. Ricci wanted to know what precinct Corvi was at, who his sergeant was. "Whoo-eee," he said. "Get ready to have your balls busted, that's all I'm gonna say." Then he remembered himself and turned the conversation back to the fire. Still holding my hand, Corvi told Ricci who I was and that we had just arrived at the scene.

"We spent the night at my place, in Gravesend," he said. "I live with my mom, and we were up watching movies and shooting the shit." In a lower, more confidential voice: "Obviously, we had nothing to do with—with this. This is—Jesus, man, this is fucking terrible. You got any ID on the body upstairs?"

In short order, Ricci was convinced that Corvi was an earnest rookie cop, a devoted son and boyfriend, a straight-shooter. Ricci was telling Corvi to look him up so they could grab a beer sometime, when my father stood up, veins popping at his temples.

"That's it?" Dad yelled. "You're going to let this punk go? He's got a reputation—" and Ricci was holding up a hand saying, "Sir. Sir. I have to ask you to calm down. Officer Welliver just arrived at the scene and has an alibi that we can easily check. So, I'll ask you to please let us do our jobs—" and it was clear that Corvi had won this brief but very important fight. There wasn't going to be another round. Corvi's downcast eyes and solemn expression betrayed no victory as he told Ricci he'd look him up, and said to my father that he was taking me to Gravesend and would look after me. He only let me in on the joke by squeezing my hand, several times, tightly.

I heard the same subtle, honeyed addition to Corvi's tone while he spoke on the phone.

"... Ah, yeah, of course. Well, I'll come by with Analie, and she can watch Brook while we're gone and stick around in case there's a call or... Okay. We'll be there as soon as we can. No, no problem, man. I'm sure it'll be fine, yeah." Corvi hung up without saying goodbye and turned towards me. His expression was serious, but an almost imperceptible smile tugged at the corners of his mouth. He became aware of it, and the smile disappeared so seamlessly, it was like had never really been there in the first place.

"That was Barrett," he said somberly. "Mia's missing."

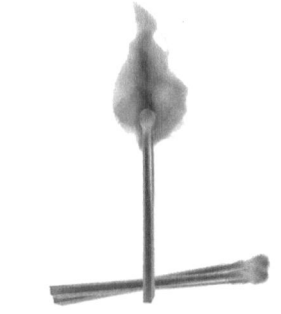

VI.
Gonzo Alonzo

1.

Corvi, visiting me at the playground in full uniform, was an event. All eyes—the nannies, the mommies, and one old guy, probably a grandfather—were on me as I scooped up Brook and walked to the entrance to greet my husband, who stood with his hands on his hips, waiting for me and at the same time scanning the area as if he might pull out his nightstick and beat someone to death at any moment. I gave him a loving, wifely kiss on the mouth so that everyone would know that this wasn't official police business. He was mine. I wasn't being arrested.

"Hey, baby," he said, and then he leaned over and squinted at Brook. "Hi, buddy."

The driver of the squad car waved to me from the window, and I waved back.

"This is nice," I said. "Is there any news—"

"Nope," he said. He pulled a pack of gum from his pocket and removed a stick of it, tearing off the foil and putting the gum in his mouth. "Just swinging by after interviewing someone in Brighton Beach. I was hoping I'd see you here." Corvi looked around for a trash can and then shoved the foil into his pocket. His eyes were red and his skin was overlaid with a sheen of perspiration. He always looked like that now.

Brook wanted to touch Corvi's badge. "Lemme have him," said Corvi, and I handed Brook over. Brook went agreeably enough, and I watched Corvi hold him up, gazing at him as though he were looking at one of the baboons at the Prospect Park Zoo. *He looks like one of us*, I could imagine he was thinking. Corvi scratched at Brook's back.

"He ain't a puppy, Motorhead." The driver had emerged from the car. He was huge, way taller than Corvi, heavyset and soft-looking, with a dark mustache, sideburns, and wire-framed glasses. "He's a *baby*. You don't *scratch* him like that."

Motorhead was Corvi's new nickname among his fellow officers. They all had nicknames, most of them ridiculous. I wasn't sure how Corvi had gotten his.

"Analie, this is my new partner, Duffy. Duffy, this is my wife, Analie." Corvi's tone was flat and pointedly unenthusiastic. Instead of just shaking my hand, Duffy clasped it in both of his and gave me a bright, winning smile.

"Tell him, Analie," he said. "Tell him he needs to take some childcare classes if he's ever going to be a dad."

"Guy has one kid and he thinks he's an expert," said Corvi disdainfully. "Hey, Duffy, maybe he *likes* having his back scratched. Huh? You like that, buddy?" Brook pouted, and Duffy laughed.

"You gotta keep your eye on him," said Duffy to me, jerking a thumb in Corvi's direction. "You guys ain't planning on starting a family, are you? I'm not sure he's father material. Don't want him whipping out the jack every time the kid spills his milk."

"Shut up, Duff."

Out of the corner of my eye I saw some of the adults at the playground look over at us again. Duffy wasn't finished busting Corvi's chops. "Do you know how he spends his time on the beat, Analie? I've never *seen* such things." Corvi snorted at this. "Kickin' in doors, bustin' up people's shit, and hittin' 'em on the back of the head if they say boo. I'm talkin' men, women, mommas, grandmaws, grand-dads... They do not want to piss this guy off. Every skel in the precinct knows it. Now imagine that you guys have a little Corvus Welliver, Jr. running around the house. He scribbles on the wall, or knocks over your family heirloom, crystal vase, what-have-you. What's Dad gonna do? Is he gonna put Junior in the corner to think about what he's done? Or drag him into lockup and beat his ass with a telephone book?" Corvi continued chewing gum and grinned widely, as if Duffy was paying him a compliment.

"That's not funny," I snapped.

Brook started squirming—Corvi was holding him strangely, and he was uncomfortable—and I took him back into my arms and kissed him on the top of his head. Corvi's hand drifted back to his nightstick.

"All right, that's enough," Corvi said again to Duffy, but Duffy went on, undaunted.

"You're worried I'm gonna make her think twice," he said. "*Hmmm, maybe I don't want this lunatic fathering my child. She* gonna turn cold on you, son. You'll be sleeping on the couch."

"Ah, she can't resist my magic fingers," said Corvi. He held his hand up, wiggling it.

"Ugh, Corvi," I hissed.

"Stop, I can't hear that shit, please." Duffy made a face. "Send me to prison instead. Put me in the gas chamber. I don't wanna hear nothin' about Motorhead's sex life."

"*Hasta luego,*" I said, shaking my head and waving them off. "You shouldn't be allowed at a playground, either of you. Duffy, so nice to meet you."

"The pleasure is all mine," said Duffy.

Corvi kissed me fiercely, leaving a bitter taste on my mouth.

"Everything okay, Analie?" He gave me a long, searching look.

Duffy, circling around the squad car and opening the door, called out mockingly.

"Yeah, everything okay?"

"Jesus Christ, mind your own fucking business, Duffy," Corvi snapped. "You're like a goddamn *woman*." He waited until Duffy was safely out of earshot before leaning close again, speaking huskily into my ear. "Okay, baby. I love you." He gave me one more kiss and then climbed into the car, shooting me a longing look. "Bye, honey."

"Bye, honey," called out Duffy, and as they peeled off I caught sight of Corvi shaking his head and reaching for the glove compartment, probably for cigarettes.

I started to wind the afternoon down, packing up the toy cars I'd brought to the playground, the container of bubbles. I gave Brook one car to hold. As I walked back to the Barrett's, pushing Brook in his stroller, I straightened up and looked straight ahead. Even after three months, walking this way—safe in my own world, not looking over my shoulder every second or seeing things out of the corner of my eye—was still exhilarating.

The day Mia went missing, I was moving slowly, groggy from the night before at Adán's office. I had a hard time remembering anything that had happened, and as the days went on, I remembered even less. Corvi drove me to the Barrett's that morning, and then back home in the evening, and I was alone for the first time the next day when I went to the bodega to buy milk. On impulse, I detoured on the way home. I passed the mailbox, on the corner of Adán's street, with the scrawled graffiti that had fascinated me as a child: *If I knew you I would love you.* I had always wanted to be known and loved, and Corvi had given me that. I knew he would do anything for me.

Adán was on his stoop, sitting and drinking coffee as though anticipating my arrival.

"*Buenas dias*, Analie."

"Hola," I said, feeling shy.

"*Como estas?*"

"Oh, things are *muy loco*," I replied. I told him that Mia was missing. "That's the mom of the little boy I take care of," I added when I saw him frown slightly.

"Missing... how?"

"Like, a couple of days ago Mia left the apartment in the morning and she never showed up for her job, and she hasn't come home."

"That's terrible," said Adán. "I guess we should—hope

for the best. And what about your friend?" He raised an eyebrow at me, smiling broadly. "Seen her lately?"

He was talking about Tenny. I felt my lips part as I struggled with the answer. I had hardly been in Gravesend the previous day. Still, she always found me. She was always around. On days I didn't leave the house, the smell of her made its way into the apartment wafting in as though she lived behind the walls. She was impossible to avoid.

But I hadn't seen her yet that morning—more importantly, I hadn't *felt* her.

"Oh my God," I breathed, and Adán kept grinning, revealing his sharp incisors. "You did it. You made her go away. Did you? Is she really gone?" He nodded. "Oh my God," I said again, and Adán laughed. I had an impulse to jump up and race home and run through the garage and into the fallout shelter, to see if she was there. "Is she—is she okay?" I asked hesitantly. "I mean, did she— where is—"

"She's fine," said Adán. "Don't worry about her. She's moved on, as she should have a long time ago."

My eyes were filling with tears. I wanted to bubble over, to say *Oh my God* a few more times, to tell Adán he was amazing, maybe even hug him. Instead, I just whispered, "Thank you."

"You're very welcome. Now, let's move on as well." His gaze was fixed on me as he sipped his coffee. He smiled at me warmly, but his eyes were cold.

"Wait," I said, trying to find words. I didn't want to sound ungrateful. "Did—anyone get hurt because of it? This doesn't have anything to do with Mia, does it?"

"Who—the woman you work for? Adán's brow creased.

"My God, no. Of course not. It's a terrible thing, though. I hope she turns up, for the sake of her little boy."

"Okay," I said, exhaling. "Thank you. I'm sorry. I just wanted to make sure. How can we ever, like, repay you? What do you even—charge for something like this?"

"Your husband's taking care of that," Adán said. "Enjoy your day, Miss Analie."

I practically ran home. My heart was pounding—whatever happened in the next few minutes felt like the most important thing in the world. I went in through the garage entrance and stood there, taking deep breaths. Mild gasoline smell, nothing else. No smoke. I almost whimpered out loud with fear and anticipation as I approached the old fallout shelter and flung the door open.

Not only was it empty, it looked empty and dusty, like no one had been inside it for years.

"Oh, thank God," I said out loud. My eyes filled with tears again. Tears of gratitude, of relief. "Thank God, thank God." I kept saying it as I made my way to the elevator, sniffling, smiling, wiping at my eyes. I couldn't wait to tell Corvi.

2.

"A real salt-of the-earth kinda guy," was how Reese described Corvi after meeting him for the first time. That was soon after I had started as Brook's nanny, on a night when I worked late. Corvi came to pick me up and take me out to dinner. Brook was asleep in bed, and Reese and Mia stood anxiously in the foyer waiting for Corvi to arrive. They were as excited to meet him as if I was their daughter on prom night, and Corvi was my date. Even though I was excited too, to show Corvi off and finally introduce him to the Barretts, I also felt bad—it was a little like an ambush. When I opened the door and Corvi saw Reese and Mia standing there expectantly, he looked dismayed.

"Hey, man, how's it going?" Reese stepped forward and he and Corvi exchanged a manly handshake. "Good to finally meet you."

"Hey," said Corvi, and then he dutifully shook hands with Mia. "Corvi. How're you doing."

"It's wonderful to meet you," said Mia. "It's been so nice knowing we have a police officer in the family."

Corvi looked confused. Like, whose family was she talking about? We weren't part of *their* family.

"New York's finest," said Reese, grinning. "I bet there's never a dull moment."

"You'd be surprised," said Corvi. He was wearing a sweatshirt that day, I remember, that said NYPD on it. He was probably sorry he'd chosen that one.

"How long have you been on the job? You're so young."

"Long enough," said Corvi. His affect was flat. He wasn't trying to charm them, which surprised me. But they seemed won over anyway.

"You must have some stories," Reese said. "Hey, how about we leave the ladies here and go out for a beer, you and me?"

Reese, Mia, and I all laughed on cue at his little joke. Corvi's eyes were starting to brighten, and he cocked his head like a cat who had just noticed a mouse. I gave his arm a tug.

"We'll let you go," said Mia, putting her arm around Reese. "Otherwise this guy's gonna keep you here all night."

"Oh, Jesus fucking Christ," Corvi said the moment we were out the door. I shushed him, imagining the Barretts listening from high above, their faces sticking out of the open window. Corvi lowered his voice, making it deep and sonorous, doing a good imitation of Reese. "'Hey, man. How's it going? How long have you been on the job?' What a fucking asshole. 'New York's finest!'"

I could see what Corvi objected to. It wasn't just Reese's appropriation of Corvi's job, his playing with the lingo, it was his appropriation of Corvi himself—Reed's assumption that he knew who Corvi was just from hearing about him and now meeting him.

"A real salt-of the-earth kinda guy," Reese said the following morning when I arrived for work. He was seeing what he wanted to see: the trustworthy Latina nanny, married too young, who they graced with a paycheck. And Corvi, a cop, a real good guy.

I tried to forgive Reese for stripping us down into the people he could feel proud of. After all, he and Mia needed to be happy with their choices. They had put me in charge of the light of their life. They had to trust me.

3.

Brook had fussed when I put him in his stroller, and threw out the little toy car I had given him. But he was mollified when I handed him some cut-up pieces of fruit in a container. The exterior of the Barrett's apartment building, as I approached, looked dull and washed out. It was like Mia's absence had stripped the life out of everything she'd touched. As he always did when we entered the building,

Brook craned his neck up at me and said made a garbled sound that sounded like it began with an M. and I said, "Not today, Brooky. I'm sorry." Their mailbox in the lobby, with BARRETT written on it in Mia's hand, was like a bad joke.

Reese was home already, even though it was early afternoon. He was doing that a lot—lingering around the apartment, wanting to be with Brook, leaving late for work and coming home early. I had just put my key in the lock when I felt movement from the other side, and Reese was opening the door.

"Hey, hey, guys. I'm so glad to see you," he said. "I was getting worried." No more *Como estás?* or throwing Brook into the air. All of that had been knocked out of him. He'd been humbled and now held everything and everyone close to him, earnestly. I was still standing in the doorway as Reese unbuckled Brook from the stroller and lifted him up into a tight embrace. "Did you guys go to the playground?"

Reese still asked Brook questions, and I answered.

"We did. We blew bubbles, we went on the swing..."

"Did you blow bubbles? Did you?" Brook said nothing, remaining impassive, his lower lip protruding in a pout. "Analie, is your husband working tonight? You're welcome to stay and have dinner with us. I'm just scrambling up eggs. You know, a real gourmet meal."

"Aw, thanks." I hesitated for just a moment, and then said, "I'd love to."

Reese smiled with relief.

After almost three months of Mia being gone, I was still tentative around this Reese. He was new to me, a Reese who sometimes broke down into tears, a heroic Reese who did everything in the household himself, who invited me to stay for dinner and then sometimes, if I hesitated, said *Please, Analie.* And then, hastily: *I mean, if you're not doing something else.* Even his smile was different. When I met him, every smile had been decisive, a choice. The result was something close-mouthed, creamy, and polished. Now he hardly smiled at all but when he did, it caught him off guard and his face became open and raw. I'd never noticed the way his full upper lip turned up at the edges, exposing just the edges of his pink gums.

He had other people for a little while. His parents visited, and were quiet and ineffectual. Reese's Dad was tall, like him, and his mother was tiny and wore neat, dark clothes and some kind of brooch with golden letters that spelled ART. Mia's mother and her stepfather flew in from Colorado and demanded to get updates from the police detectives who were working the case. A housekeeper named Lupé who came once a week and said to me, under her breath and in Spanish, "He says he doesn't know where she is. You be careful, Analie" before turning to Reese and giving him a simple smile that reassured him, every time he saw it, that he was in the presence of yet another benign, protective, loyal domestic. ("I hope you can help me *communicate* better with Lupay," Mia had told me brightly when I'd started.) There was even a friend of Mia's, another mom, who came by from time to time with what I perceived to be a sort of appraisal of Reese and Brook, as though she were ready to pounce on what had been Mia's once, what still might be Mia's, if only anyone knew what had happened to her.

The police hadn't seemed too concerned at first, although by the time I arrived at work that first morning after she disappeared, Reese was panicking. "I don't understand," he kept saying to me. "Where is she? What could have possibly happened?"

I stayed at the apartment with Brook, waiting for Mia to call, or walk through the door, and Reese spent hours at the police station talking to detectives. Corvi called sometimes at the Barrett's to tell me something or ask me a question, but I knew it was to check in. One foot in his world, and trying to get a foothold in mine. Corvi, against a background of talking, ringing telephones, and the general chaos at the precinct. "I need you to settle something for me"—then to someone else—"I'm asking her right now, shut up! Sorry"—focused on me again—"That plane crash back a million years ago, it was two planes, right? One crashed in Park Slope, the other in Staten Island, right? Right. The Park Slope plane crash and the Miller Field crash. Same day. I told you guys"—this to his fellow officers, who yelled back at him belligerently—"I swear to God you're like trolls living under a bridge. Just listen to me when I tell you something, okay? They *collided*. What, you think they just dropped out of the sky 'cause they ran out of gas?" And then, suddenly speaking to me again: "You doing okay?"

When Reese came home from meeting with the detectives, in his t-shirt and sweatpants, he smelled sweaty. I wondered what the police had thought of him. Did they know that on a good day, he was hearty and impeccable in his suits, with his combed-back sandy hair and deep voice? "They think I'm confused," he said, pushing his hair back from his face, shaking his head. "They said she must have gone on a business trip or something. They asked me if she'd ever been *unfaithful*."

"They have to ask that, Reese—"

They asked me too, when days had passed and it became clear something was very wrong.

"To your knowledge, was Mrs. Barrett involved with anyone else romantically? The last time you saw her, did you see anything unusual, did she have any large bags with her, anything like that?"

I shook my head.

"What was her mood like?"

"It was just—normal. Just rushed, but—fine. Really."

"And did she say or do anything out-of-the-ordinary?"

"No, just—she said they'd overslept and she was running late—"

"Why did they oversleep?"

"I don't know. I didn't—she just said it."

"Did you see her leave?"

"Yeah, I mean—no, I didn't see her walk out the door, but I heard her say goodbye, and then the door open and close."

"And you don't know why they were running late?"

No, I repeated emphatically. How would I? But the detectives fixed on that, they wanted to know more from Reese. Why was Mia late that morning? Had they argued? Been up late the night before? Any alcohol or drugs?

"Husband's the first one they suspect," said Corvi almost smugly when we talked about it. "And he's the last known person to see her alive? Forget about it. He's got no one to corroborate anything he says. Guy's fucked."

"But it's Reese," I said plaintively. "You know him. He literally would not hurt a fly. He doesn't even eat meat."

Corvi shrugged. "That's what he *wants* everyone to think."

But I didn't believe it. Even if he'd gone temporarily

insane and murdered his wife, and then pulled himself back together and gone to work first thing in the morning, there was no way that Reese could pretend to be as baffled as he was in the days and weeks following Mia's disappearance—the way he trailed off in mid-sentence, forgetting his words, making mistakes like buying a carton of buttermilk instead of skim milk, staying up nights on the couch by the window.

Mia's mother looked just like her, and her stepfather had a big white beard and wore red bow ties. "Reese and Mia tell us you're just about perfect," he said to me one afternoon as we all sat awkwardly around the living room. His name was Bill or Bob—I could never remember. "In fact, the only drawback they can think of is that you haven't agreed to be Brook's nanny for life."

I gave him a little smile.

"Oh, I'd agree to it in a heartbeat," I said. "But Brook isn't going to need me forever. He'll probably be ready to take care of himself the day he starts kindergarten."

Bill-or-Bob held up his hand and wagged a finger.

"No, no, bite your tongue. We're in no hurry for him to grow up."

God, what were we even talking about? I didn't even know, the platitudes were making me feel like I was going to gag. I glanced over at Reese.

He was staring into space, his expression blank.

"... and he's not going to grow up without his momma. We will not let that happen," finished Bill-or-Bob with a catch in his throat. Mia's mother wiped her eyes. Reese stood up suddenly and left the room. I wanted to go after him, but I felt like everyone was staring at me. I waited a few minutes and then started clearing coffee mugs and little plates and crumpled-up napkins, and after I'd brought it all to the kitchen, I went to the door of Reese and Mia's bedroom, and I knocked.

No one answered. I cracked the door open anyway and slipped in, closing it behind me. Reese was sitting on the edge of the bed, his head in his hands. He looked up when I entered.

"Analie, thank God it's you," he said. I went to him and then knelt down in front of him. "I feel like I'm losing my mind."

I patted him on the knee. I didn't know what to say.

"I don't understand how everyone can just—sit around, drinking coffee and just—*bullshitting* like this, when we don't know where she is. How can they stand it? I can't. I mean I—really—can't—bear it—" He put his face in his hands again. "What if she's—what if she's hurt, or someone is—mistreating her—"

"Reese," I said helplessly, and then I sat down beside him and put my arms around his neck. To my surprise, he hugged me back immediately, burying his warm face in my neck, crying openly.

"The time is just—ticking away," he choked out. "And I can't stop it. I can't stop it for her, or for me, or for Brook—"

"Shhhhh," I murmured, shifting so I fit better alongside him, patting him on the back. "You're doing everything you can. The police are on it. We're going to find her, Reese." I did believe it, that she'd be found. I just wasn't sure what that meant.

"Thank you," he whispered. "You're so good, Analie. I would be absolutely lost without you."

You're so good, Analie.

I went over it over and over when I finally walked home. I loved those words. I loved being good. But it felt like something I needed to hold onto, something that wasn't a part of me, like an article of clothing that might be snatched away from me at any moment.

4.

After Mia disappeared, Corvi was transferred to a precinct in Bed-Stuy, the 77. It wasn't a good thing. There didn't seem to be anywhere safe in New York City, but Bed-Stuy was like the apocalypse Tenny and I had imagined all those years ago when we ate jellybeans in the old fallout shelter. Burned-out buildings, vacant houses, hills made of rubble—it was something out of a nightmare, and knowing that Corvi was there day after day, night after night, made me feel ill. I imagined horrible things—a shootout, a robbery gone bad, Corvi slashed by a crazed, drug-addled druggie. I thought of all the terrible things that can happen to a police officer. And meanwhile, I went to work as usual, I pushed Brook around in his stroller, I spooned out his yogurt, I sliced a pear that when I tasted it turned out to be so good, so ripe, that I ate it myself instead of giving it to him. I answered the detectives' questions, looking at their faces for an indication of—something. But there was nothing there, they were consistently unsmiling, almost bored-looking. I watched Reese, saw the peculiar mingling of hope and panic on his face whenever the phone rang. And when it was time for me to go home, I raced back to Gravesend and hoped that I'd fling open our apartment door and find Corvi stretched out on the couch and waiting for me. He usually wasn't, of course. He continued with his strange hours and never seemed to be clear on what his schedule would be like.

Valdez was the one who told me about Corvi's transfer. One night I was sitting on the couch, staring into space, thinking about everyone—Mia, Reese, Brook, Corvi—when I heard a scuffling outside our door and then the doorbell rang. My stomach lurched. I jumped up and, without checking the peephole, unlocked the door and flung it open to find Valdez, in his uniform, supporting Corvi, who was also in his blues. Corvi's face was shiny with sweat and his eyes focused on mine, briefly.

"I'm just really tired," he said by way of explanation, and then his head lolled back. I stood back wordlessly and let them in. Valdez surveyed the living room and then deposited Corvi on the nearest couch, bending over him and folding Corvi's hands neatly over his waist as if preparing a corpse for a wake.

"What happened?"

"Whooo," said Valdez. He stood up straight and stretched, trying to catch his breath. "Analie, you got a cold one?"

"Are you serious?"

Valdez gave me a look. "As serious as a heart attack. No glass necessary, straight from the can will do." I sighed heavily and went into the kitchen, pulling a beer out of the fridge and bringing it back to Valdez. He cracked it open and took a long swig, and then said, "Whooo," again. "Sit, Analie."

I sat.

"Do you know why Corvi's nickname is Motorhead?"

I shook my head no.

"It's a term for, like, a car fanatic—"

"I know what a motorhead is."

"Okay, well, we like to call him that because he, uh—well, he likes to tune people up." He looked at me closely to see if I understood. "We say in the precinct that when you beat the living holy hell outta someone, you're tunin' them up. And he's so good at tune-ups, he's like a mechanic. A motorhead."

"Isn't that what cops do on the job?"

"Nah, not like this. He'll fuck anyone up and he doesn't hold back. He's big on using the jack. Skels see him coming down the block swinging that thing, they take off. Which is good in its own way, don't get me wrong. The review board gets complaints about him, but he's always managed to talk his way outta trouble. You know Corvi. Well, the last few months he's gotten worse... and last night he was full-on mental. Went straight to the locker room where there was some drinking and stuff going on, and was three sheets before we even stepped foot inside the squad car. Then, later —you didn't hear it from me, but Corvi and I, uh, we did some coke..."

"*What?*"

"It happens sometimes, Analie. These tours just go on forever. And you gotta be sharp. Do you know how many times we go head-to-head with someone who would just as soon see us dead? Not only that, but we gotta cover our own asses every second. Guy tries to escape out the back window, falls three stories, and breaks both his legs, next thing you know he's saying the cops pushed him. You don't know what it's like out there. You're up against the bad guys and they just keep coming and meanwhile, if they get you, you're *out*.

As in, dead or fucked up for life. The coke helps if you do even a little bump. Really makes you sharp."

"Corvi's never said anything about that," I interjected.

"Well, I don't tell Stacey about it neither," Valdez shot back. "Listen. We got called to a domestic dispute, Corvi kicks the door in, and there was this fucking jackass in a suit and tie doing lines on a glass table. Corvi smacks him around a little and then samples the coke, says it's great. I did a bump too. The suit starts mouthing off, saying we're stealing his stuff, blah blah blah, and Corvi grabs him by the back of the head and starts smashing his face into the glass table."

"Fuck," I said.

"Yeah, well, eventually he busted up the table, but kept it up, and the suit's face got cut to ribbons. Something happened with the guy's eye, it caught on a shard of glass? A chunk got pulled right out of its socket—"

"Oh my God."

"—And Corvi's doing more of the coke! I mean, I've got his back, I'll say the guy jumped him, resisted arrest and so on, but this isn't gonna go down well with the brass. It wasn't some skel, it was a privileged middle-aged white guy who's having himself a night. And then there's a witness, the girl who dropped the dime in the first place. Guy got rough with her, she calls us, then she's standing there screaming bloody murder the whole time. It was just a fucking mess. Luckily, she was a hooker, so her word don't mean shit, and somehow by the grace of God, Corvi didn't get drug tested. He had a leprechaun up his ass in that regard, for sure. By the time they get around to it, he'll come up clean or he can get some rookie to take a piss for him. But there's no getting around the fact that this fucking suit's missing a piece of his eye and is gonna be scarred for life..."

"What's going to happen? Is Corvi fired?"

"Nah, but they're gonna move him. To the 77 in Bed-Stuy. I gotta tell you, Analie. It's a dumping ground for the guys who fuck up. And it's a bad place for him. They call it the Alamo."

We stared at each other. Finally, I said, "Thanks, Valdez."

"I'm probably not gonna see Corvi for a while, Analie. Or you, for that matter."

"I get it."

"But tell him this'll go away. I'm just sorry they're splitting us up and sending him to the 77. Like I said, it's—it's not gonna be good for him. Maybe he'll want to think about getting out. You know, there are places around the country that pay good money to hire NYPD, right? Nice towns in the Midwest. I'm serious. You guys could move there and you won't be smack in the middle of this fucking city. Maybe Corvi should put in some applications. Quick, before any of this shit comes down."

"Thanks, Valdez," I said again, coldly. I couldn't help but feel like it was Valdez's job to keep an eye on Corvi and he hadn't really done a good job. Valdez was his partner, for Christ's sake. What had he been doing while Corvi was pummeling the guy into the glass table? Just standing there, no doubt, with one thumb up his ass—as Corvi would say—and a finger-full of coke in his nose.

Valdez seemed to know what I was thinking. He was silent as I walked to the door and opened it, waiting for him to leave.

126

"Have his uniform dry-cleaned," said Valdez. His parting words. "It's got a lot of blood on it."

As soon as he was gone, I went to the couch and knelt down beside Corvi. He was asleep, breathing hard, his hands still folded over his waist. I thought about little boy Corvi. The days and nights didn't get easier, did they? If children like him—unhappy and powerless—knew how hard life was going to be, night after night after night, they'd probably all kill themselves before they turned twelve. Did a happy childhood exist, and was it meant to act as a buffer for when life comes crashing down? And then if life *didn't* crumble like some kind of enormous mudslide or avalanche, what did that mean? Maybe that it was only a dream that the privileged rested their heads on, slumbering while the rest of us struggled to find peace, to breathe. I hated how some people got to live in that dream. My only consolation was that almost always, unhappiness had to creep in somewhere, like an infection, and spread until the whole dream was corrupted. I knew that now. Anyone could get it. The richest, the whitest. Maybe they were just more surprised when it happened to them—sickness, addiction, suicide, ruin. They said things like *We've had a good life* and *We'll get through this.* But also *Why?* and *I never thought this could happen to us.*

Fuck them, I thought savagely.

I was *glad* that bad things happened to those people.

Reese and Mia—could they ever have imagined what lay ahead?

I almost laughed out loud. And in this quiet, private moment—in my own head—I acknowledged it.

I was happy about what had happened to the Barretts.

Mia gone, the new, vulnerable Reese.

None of it would be real if things had kept going their way. It was like their life, so high up before, had tilted towards me like a see-saw and allowed me to climb on.

And it made me happy.

I put my hands on either side of Corvi's sweaty face, and I kissed his mouth. He didn't wake up. I knew all of this was taking something from him, even if I didn't understand why. I'd never asked what Adán had charged us for his magic, for making Tenny disappear. I guessed it was money, and that was why Corvi was working more and numbing himself every single way he knew how—drinking, drugging, beating people up. He didn't laugh as much anymore. But it was more than debt that was eating away at him. Still, I never brought it up. I didn't want to ask him what he owed Adán because I didn't want to owe Adán anything, too.

5.

Reese burned the eggs. I was sitting in the living room, mindlessly building and rebuilding a block tower so that Brook could knock it down over and over, when I smelled food burning. I got up, leaving Brook to play with the blocks on his own, and went into the kitchen. Reese was standing in front of the stove with a spatula, looking down at the smoking pan and crying.

"Hey," I said. I reached over and turned off the burner, then put my hand over his, guiding it until he held the spatula over the sink. It fell with an ugly clattering sound. I put my arms around his waist and hugged him. Reese's body was different than Corvi's, much softer. He was tall and slim, but his occasional runs, bike rides, or games of basketball with his buddies hadn't keep his body hard in the same way that Corvi's routine did. Corvi, who was always running, struggling, leaping, training, stretching, pumping his fists into thin air, boxing an invisible foe, jogging in place... Corvi who could barely stay still unless we were in bed together asleep. In sleep, he always looked absolutely exhausted, almost lifeless. That was how much he moved when he was awake.

Reese hugged me back, pressing his face into my hair. I released him slightly, but he was still holding on to me, so I tightened my arms again. Brook sounded content enough from the other room. I could hear blocks being stacked and then scattered, over and over. At first, I was comforting Reese, but then I found myself relaxing into his body as he held me. He ran his hand along my hair, drifting down to my shoulders, then back up to my temple, starting all over again. I had a sudden realization—an awareness that rapidly became heart-pounding and bright. Sure enough, his hands gently turned my face up to his, his mouth found mine and —we were kissing.

The sound of the buzzer startled the crap out of both of us. I gasped and stepped backward, looking toward the intercom as if it might reveal the identity of this unexpected visitor. Reese's eyes were wide, and he lunged forward and pressed the button marked TALK. "Hello?"

"Mr. Barrett?" The voice on the other end was fuzzy, almost unintelligible. Underneath the layers of cognizance —*Reese and I just kissed, is Brook okay in the other room, there's someone ringing the buzzer*—it occurred to me that I had never, in my lifetime of living in New York, encountered an intercom system where the voice on the other end was clear.

Reese fumbled with the buttons.

"Yes," he said, looking at me with panic in his eyes.

"It's Detectives Purcell and Massey. Can we come up?"

Wordlessly, Reese pressed the button to let them in. His face was pale and getting paler right in front of me.

"Oh, my God," he whispered.

"No, no," I said urgently. "It doesn't have to be bad news. Maybe they just want to ask you something—Reese—"

Brook started crying.

I pushed past Reese and went into the living room, scooping up Brook just as the doorbell rang. Then I darted over to the door and opened it for the detectives.

I knew Purcell, he'd been there that first day Mia was missing. Massey was shorter than Purcell, with thick eyebrows that met in the middle.

"Hi," I whispered.

Purcell nodded at me and then said to Massey, "The nanny." Massey met my eyes briefly and then looked down. They stepped inside. "Is Mr. Barrett home?" asked Purcell.

"I'm here."

We all turned toward Reese, who stood at the doorway of the kitchen, leaning against the doorframe. His face was white, and he looked like he was about to keel over.

I jiggled Brook in my arms. That was something about babies—they were always *there*, whether you wanted them to be or not. It would have been so much more convenient for Brook to be sleeping, but he wasn't. He was wide awake and hungry for dinner.

"Mr. Barrett, let's have a seat," said Purcell. Smoothly, Massey guided Reese over to the dinner table, where Purcell pulled out one of the chairs. Reese sat down, his eyes wide.

We all took turns looking at each other. "We need to talk to you," said Purcell with a significant glance at me. "Perhaps your, uh, nanny would like to take the child into the other room?"

"What's happened?" whispered Reese, ignoring the question. I ignored it too. I tried to put Brook in his seat but he let out a scream. I looked wildly around, spied a calculator on top of a pile of papers on Reese's desk, and grabbed it. I gave it to Brook and successfully got him to sit in his high chair. Heart pounding, I found myself imagining, in what seemed like just a fraction of a second, what would happen if Mia was dead. It was amazing how much imagery could come to mind in a fraction of a second. Brook stopped crying while he examined the calculator.

"Good trick," said Massey, and he gave me a small smile.

"Mr. Barrett, I believe we've found your car," said Purcell. "I'm going to show you some photographs, but there's something I need to tell you first—"

"You've found—the car? What about Mia?"

Purcell shook his head. "There was no sign of her—"

"Where was it?"

"Brownsville."

"In *Brownsville*?"

Their words were overlapping, and my eyes darted between the two men. Massey was watching them, too, with a critical expression on his face.

"Mr. Barrett, can you think of any reason your wife would have been in that area?"

"No," said Reese. "We've certainly never been there."

Massey made a face. It was almost imperceptible, but I

saw it, and it made me wince a little bit. "Why do you need to show me pictures? Don't you have the license plate—"

"The license plates were damaged," Purcell said. "The car was set on fire. But we were able to get some partial numbers that we believe are a match."

I inhaled, sharply. My ears buzzed and the back of my neck prickled all over. My face suddenly felt hot, as though I were standing in front of the car as it burned.

"The car was set on fire?" asked Reese, his mouth hanging open.

Brook threw the calculator on the floor with a yell.

"Excuse me," I said, and I went into the kitchen. My hands were shaking as I pulled a block of cheese out of the refrigerator, and a bag of peas from the freezer. I turned the oven on and while it heated, I chopped up some cheese and put the frozen peas in a bowl. When I brought them out, the three men were in the exact same positions I had left them. I placed the food in front of Brook, who began to eat voraciously.

"Are those peas *frozen*?" asked Massey. "You give 'em to him like that?"

"He loves it," I said, my voice quavering.

"I'll have to try that with my youngest," said Massey. "He's a real picky eater."

"I don't understand," Reese said. "When did all this happen?"

"It seems the car was found burning on the same day that your wife went missing," said Purcell. "But we didn't make the connection—"

"Wait, the car was found—three months ago? And you're just figuring it out now?"

"You have to understand, we weren't looking for the car or your wife in Brownsville," said Purcell almost kindly. "A burned-out car there is not exactly news. And with the license plates being damaged, well, putting it together right away was kind of a long shot. It just so happens that we got a guy who was running plate numbers for another case and he made the connection. We're still not even sure—so before we go on, I'm going to show you some pictures. The car is badly damaged but I just want to know if anything jumps out at you."

I saw that Brook was nearing the end of his peas, so I went into the kitchen. I took fish sticks out of the freezer, threw them on a baking tray, and put them in the oven. I set a timer that was shaped like a chicken, grabbed another fistful of frozen peas, and brought them back to the table, where I dropped them into Brook's bowl. Reese was staring at the photographs that Purcell had handed to him. It made me think of Valdez and his envelope of photos, and Corvi's grinning face next to the yellowish-whitish, nibbled-at hunk of matter that was once a person.

"Can you tell us the make and model of your car again, Mr. Barrett?"

Reese looked up with an incredulous expression. "What, did you forget? I told you. It's a 1978 Buick Electra 225. Beige."

"Okay. Just want to make sure. Does the car in these photographs look like your car?"

Reese was flipping through them over and over as though shuffling them. "Yeah, I mean—yes, it could be—"

"See the glass on the ground there? We think the perpetrator broke the rear window first, for better access to the interior. Then it appears that he—or she—specifically poured accelerant in the front and rear exterior of the car to destroy the license plates. But as you can see, there are some numbers remaining here—" Purcell pointed at one picture, and then Reese flipped to another photo and Purcell went on "—and here. Do these seem to match the license plate numbers on your car?"

"Yes," said Reese quietly.

"Mr. Barrett, was your wife carrying any valuables on the morning she disappeared, or did she have a large sum of money on her person? Anything that would make her a target for someone?"

Reese was still. Then he said, "A target?"

"Like for a robbery," spoke up Massey.

I watched the color flare up in Reese's face. He suddenly stood up and threw the photos down, much like Brook had thrown the calculator earlier.

"Oh, you mean—you mean *now* you think something happened to her? Instead of her running off with someone? I told you and I told you she would never leave Brook. She would never have left me, but I know for some reason you just refused to believe that. Now, now, *now* you believe me?"

Brook had stopped eating and was staring at Reese. Both Purcell and Massey remained impassive. "Do you have a supervisor?" Reese looked around as if their sergeant might materialize out of thin air. "I want to talk to your boss. And tell him that the two of you are just—completely incompetent. You have no idea what you're doing."

"Calm down, Mr. Barrett," said Massey, but Reese put a hand on his hip and said, "Did you find any trace of her? Any—any ideas, or leads?" and Purcell said, "No."

"Then seriously, get the—get out of here," said Reese. "Now."

"Just one more question," said Purcell, and he shot a glance in my direction. "This is a little—sensitive—"

"Oh, please. Just spit it out and then go."

Purcell sighed. "Have you had a chance to think about— is there any chance, any chance at all that your wife was seeing someone else, or involved in some way in another relationship?"

"No," said Reese, gritting his teeth. "I keep telling you, neither one of us was *fucking* anyone else." I flinched. Reese went on. "Why can't you accept that and move on to, I don't know, something that's actually helpful?"

"Okay," said Massey. "We just wondered if you remembered anything—some little detail."

"We'll talk more when you've had a chance to calm down," added Purcell. The two of them nodded at me, and then they let themselves out. Just then, the timer went off, so I went into the kitchen and removed the fish sticks from the oven, and put them into a little plastic plate. I started blowing on them immediately as I walked back out to the table. Brook saw me and held his arms out, making an *Ummm-ummm* sound with his mouth. "Hold on, Brooky," I said. "It's hot-hot. Lemme cool it off."

"I think you should go, too, Analie," said Reese. One hand was still on his hip; the other was resting on the table-top. He was staring straight down. "I'll take it from here."

"Are you sure?" I was startled. I had a frightening feeling that he could see the fire in my past. Did he know? Had he known all along?

No, there was no way. It was impossible.

I set the plate of fish sticks down on the table and said, "Okay. Let me know if you need anything."

"I'll do that," said Reese. He didn't look up, or say anything when I left.

6.

I was frowning as I put my keys in the lock. Sometimes when I got home from work, Corvi would have other officers over. His new partner, Duffy, or a whole group of men. I always knew they were in the apartment the second I stepped off the elevator. I could hear their voices, and the hallway was thick with their cigarette smoke—not, thankfully, the same smell as when Tenny had been around—and it made the hall seem stifling. This time it was just Duffy.

"Wifey's home," I heard Duffy say when I walked in, and Corvi said, "About time."

Two pairs of extremely reddened eyes focused on me when I entered the living room. Both guys were wasted—on what, I wasn't sure. Corvi was sitting on the couch in an undershirt and jeans, and Duffy sat across from him in my Abuela's old armchair, wearing slacks and a plaid button down shirt that was unbuttoned at the top and revealing his hairy chest. Both men had cigarettes clamped in their mouths. The coffee table in front of them was covered with crumpled bills in various denominations.

"What's happening here?" I asked, dismayed. The apartment felt foreign to me—maybe I was thinking about how it had been in my childhood, everything clean and polished, the air filled with a blend of the fragrance of my Abuela's perfume with the scent of her cooking.

"Why are you home so late?" asked Corvi in a belligerent, childish way. He tried to focus his eyes on me, but they seemed to jump around. Duffy kept his eyes down as he went through the money, smoothing out each bill and sorting it all out.

"I stayed a little late and helped with dinner."

"Come on, the guy can't make fucking dinner for himself and the kid by now? What do they eat when you're not around? Dust bunnies?"

Duffy snickered.

"I need to talk to you," I said.

"Go ahead." Corvi rolled those reddened eyes at me. He gestured to Duffy. "Say whatever in front of him, we're, you know, brothers in blue."

"Corvi, can I please just talk to you?"

"Just say whatever it is, Analie," said Corvi tersely. "I can't —I don't think I can get up off the couch." With that, he and Duffy both burst into uproarious laughter. The cigarette in Duffy's mouth went flying and landed on one of the rugs— one of Abuela's rugs—where it immediately began to burn a small hole.

"Shit," said Duffy, and he dove for it, knocking a few things over in the process. Then when he picked it up, he yelped and fumbled with it for a moment before putting it out in the ashtray on the table. Corvi was laughing again but I saw him look at the hole in the rug, and the wisps of smoke that curled out of it, with a fond, dreamy look.

I felt a flush of anger rise to the tips of my ears.

"The police just came by to talk to Reese," I hissed. "They found Mia's car and it was burned out, do you think that's funny?"

Duffy made a face, an exaggerated *what is she so upset about?*

Corvi frowned.

"Who gives a shit?"

"Well, Reese does, for one thing," I said. "And I think Brook will probably grow up wondering what happened to his mother." Corvi looked unimpressed. He resumed sorting the money. "Where did you get all this money?"

"We took it," mumbled Corvi through his cigarette. "We busted in on some drug dealers—"

"They had all this shit—" Duffy chimed in.

"And like five seconds after we busted in, their customers were knocking on the door!"

"So we were like, well, it's just sitting here—

"And we sold it!"

Corvi grinned at me lopsidedly, and then squinted. He stood up so fast that money drifted off the table, disturbed by the sheer force of the air around him. Within what seemed like a split second, he lunged toward me and had his hands around my arms, holding me in place.

"What happened to you?" he hissed, right in my face.

Duffy said, "Whoa."

I tried to turn away, but Corvi grabbed my chin with one hand, forcing me to make eye contact with him. "What happened," he said again. It was like he could somehow see the imprint of the secret kiss with Reese.

"Nothing happened. I told you, the police came—"

"Not that," he said quietly. "Not that."

We stared at each other, both of us breathing hard and fast.

"Nothing, Corvi. Nothing else happened."

Duffy spoke up again. "Easy, Motorhead. Let her go."

"Fuck you," said Corvi without looking away from me.

"Let me go, please," I whispered.

Corvi grinned at me.

"Never," he said.

7.

"Can we talk about Mia's car now?" I said to Corvi when I saw him the next morning. He was sitting at the table, smoking and drinking coffee. One hand was resting on the tabletop, tapping away.

"Sure, why not?"

I folded my arms across my chest and waited for him to ask me something, anything, but he just stared at me belligerently. As he took a drag off his cigarette, he shifted in his seat and spread his legs slightly, sending me a message with his body. It was like an invitation. I met his gaze and he smirked. Without thinking about it, I rubbed at my mouth as if I was rubbing Reese's kiss off my lips.

"Don't you want to know where they found it?"

"Sure," he said, with exaggerated interest. "Where did they find it?"

"Brownsville."

"Brownsville? What was Mia doing in Brownsville? Her dainty white feet can't touch the ground in Brownsville. The heavens will weep."

"Very funny. I don't know if her feet touched the ground or not. They found her car all burned up."

"Ooooh," he said, and raised his eyebrows at me. He put

the cigarette out in the ashtray that sat in the center of the table. "So, did they find her, too?"

"No. Just the car."

"Hmmm. So, she's still gonzo alonzo. Did Reese tell you all this?"

"I was there when the detectives came over, last night. Right before I was supposed to leave."

"And? How did he take it?"

"He was—I don't know. He was angry. Because I guess the car was found burned up right after she went missing, but they didn't connect the dots until now. He told the detectives to get out." Corvi made a face to show me he was unimpressed. "They didn't take him seriously before," I went on, feeling defensive on Reese's behalf. "Well, now they know that something terrible happened."

"Oh, I don't know about *terrible*," said Corvi. "It was a Buick Electra, right? No great loss."

"Corvi—" I started, and then I shook my head. "You don't care. I get that, loud and clear. Just forget it."

"Analie, are you fucking kidding me?"

We'd never really fought, the whole time we'd been together. I'd always felt proud of that. I wanted to hold back, to not give in to the fight. But he was pissing me off. Why shouldn't I give a shit about Mia's disappearance? Why did Corvi have to see me as so awful, so uncaring, when Reese could look at me and said, *You're so good Analie.* I liked being the good Analie, and I felt like Corvi was trying to take that away from me.

"You're still a good girl, Analie," Corvi said, getting up. "You haven't done anything wrong. Not lately, at least." I was startled. It was like he'd been reading my mind. I took a step backwards as he approached me, getting closer and closer, pausing in front of me with a smile, leaning forward as though he were going to kiss me. But his eyes flicked over me and he said, "I'm gonna go back to bed, baby. I'm tired." And he kept going, walking into the bedroom, closing the door behind him. Anger flared up inside of me, I felt it as harshly as though I'd been boxed on the ears. It made me think of Reese's mouth on mine, his big, hot hands on either side of my face. I wanted to storm out of the apartment and walk straight to Midwood and ring Reese's buzzer and take the stairs and find him standing, confused, at the open door. I wanted to throw myself into his arms and finish what he'd started in the kitchen. I wanted to hear him say not just *You're so good, Analie,* but also *You feel so good* and *You make me feel so good.* And so on—goodness all around us, a bubble of it, with Corvi on the outside, locked out.

VII.
The Mechanic

I.

Corvi started driving to work regularly once he was in Bed-Stuy instead of taking the train. On the days our schedules aligned, he dropped me off at work in the mornings. Sometimes he even came up with me to check in with Reese, to shake his hand, to say *How's it going, man?* and *If there's anything I can do...* with appropriately downcast eyes and a subdued expression. I knew what he was doing—he was marking his territory, and feeling Reese out, seeing if anything had happened between us. But Reese reverted back to his aloof, polished ways. He didn't come close to me or mention the kiss at all. He didn't show his gums on the rare occasions when he smiled. At first, I was relieved. But then I started to hate him for it. So in that moment, he'd needed the physical contact, and now because he felt whatever way about it—ashamed, guilty, regretful—he pretended it hadn't happened? I hated his privilege. I had fantasies that drove him to me. It couldn't be that Mia's body was found, because that would leave him a sodden, grieving mess. No, I imagined that she was discovered on the lam with a new guy, in Miami or Los Angeles, and Reese raged about the betrayal, turning to me and telling me *I've been so stupid, Analie* and taking me in his arms, and I tried to push him away and said, *Reese, we can't.* And he said, *Goddammit, I want you. I need you. Brook does, too. You're more like a mother to him than Mia ever was* and we kissed again, finally. I didn't know what to do with Corvi in these fantasies. It wasn't enough that he was somewhere else, he needed to be dead—shot while on duty, maybe—in order to make it at all feasible. Because otherwise he came roaring into the reverie like a wild animal, tearing Reese away from me and ripping him into shreds.

And then one day Reese lingered instead of leaving for work, sitting and looking over some papers at his desk as I got Brook dressed and ready to go out. When I buckled Brook into the stroller, Reese stood and asked if he could walk with us.

"Sure," I said coolly, but I was pleased. Reese held the door for me, he hurried to the elevator and said, "Let me get that" and pushed the button. "Hey, buddy," he said to Brook. "Daddy's gonna walk with you a little, does that sound good?" Brook didn't respond or give any indication he'd heard him.

We walked outside, not speaking again until we got to the corner. And then Reese said, "Analie..."

I looked at him expectantly.

"I wanted to say—to apologize for—what happened in the kitchen—"

"Oh, no, you don't have to—"

"No, I—" Reese took a deep breath and faced me. The light had changed, but he didn't notice, and we stood at the corner like that. "I am so sorry that I—that we—I didn't mean for that to happen. You have to understand that you— your presence—for me and Brook—it's meant the world—"

"It's okay," I said, trying to stop him, but he held up his hand.

"You know, you are—you're so wonderful with Brook, and you're—very beautiful, Analie. And, you—you don't seem to know it. It makes you even more—" Reese's face was flushed, and he suddenly grinned his special smile, with the gums. "God, I'm making a total mess of this! I should not have kissed you, it was just—having you in my arms like that —and when the detectives showed up, I felt so guilty, like— whew," he said, shaking his head. "And now I've been a total asshole and all weird. So I wanted to say I'm sorry and, you know, Brook needs you. I need you. God. We can't lose you, and I—I respect the hell out of your husband, he's a great guy. I, uh, assume you didn't say anything to him, and that's why I'm still alive. I appreciate that, and it won't happen again. I promise."

I could feel myself flushing, too, and I looked down and fussed with the back of the stroller.

"It's okay," I said.

"Thanks, Analie." Reese stood there smiling at me, his white shirt making his skin look very tan and hearty. Then he leaned into Brook's stroller and gave him a kiss. "Bye, buddy," he said. "I love you. Bye, Analie. I'll see you later. And thank you."

"Sure," I said. I watched him as he strode off toward the

subway station. The conversation had warmed me, and I replayed it over and over as I slowly pushed the stroller. I wasn't even sure where I was going. The library? The playground? Should I keep going, circle the park? The walk would give me time to think while Brook stared silently out of his stroller, only occasionally squealing and holding out his hand for something to eat or drink.

I was glad I wouldn't see Corvi, I knew he'd see the warmth of that conversation on my face, in the curve of my mouth. I knew he wouldn't materialize in his squad car, because he spent far more time away from home now, at the Alamo. And he'd changed so much. He didn't burst through the door, calling for me, holding his arms open so I could bound into them. Instead, he walked in stiffly, sitting down on the sofa slowly and rubbing at his shoulders as if his limbs were hurting him. He was secretive. He didn't have as many stories to share with me, the silly or disgusting anecdotes, the suicides and the sex games gone wrong. When I came into the apartment and there were other cops there, everyone would go silent the moment I walked in the door. Duffy, his enormous frame slumped on Abuela's sofa, with his mustache and pretend-innocent eyes. A sly-looking older cop with silver hair who everyone called Denver. And Landry, who was a rookie with a baby face. The scene often reminded me of the game *What's wrong with this picture?* Once the guys had squares of cheese set up on the table, each individually wrapped, stacked like building blocks. Other times it was money. I saw them shoot glances at me, as if waiting to see if I would say something, but I never did. I tried to pretend it didn't bother me to have these men crowded into our living room, the air thick with cigarette smoke, their empties on every available space. And in some ways, it was okay, because it put a barrier between Corvi and I. It was like a wall that I could lean up against, with him on the other side doing whatever he was doing. I didn't have to really see him, so I didn't have to know what was happening or what he was going through. But in other ways it was annoying—cleaning up the beer cans after they left, opening up the windows to let the smoke clear out, not getting a chance to talk with Corvi. By the time we were alone together, Corvi would be nodding off or staring into space as he smoked one last cigarette before calling it a day, or a night, too tired to take off his clothes. He fell asleep with a burning cigarette between his fingers so often that I wondered if he wanted us to go up in flames. And he was mostly too tired for sex. Not having that contact with him meant that something was building up inside me, a reservoir that might swell up and overflow at any moment.

I wanted to tell him that he had me no matter what.

But I didn't, because I wasn't sure anymore.

I thought of the burned-out mess of a car, abandoned in Brownsville.

Had Corvi done it?

I imagined him circling the car like an animal, and then I looked at him, asleep on the couch. His blonde head, with the halo of soft gray cotton of his hoodie, looked too vulnerable to belong to someone who'd set fire to a family car, who'd disappear a mother from her family.

2.

Moira called. I'd forgotten she existed. Sometimes I wondered: if she died in her apartment, how long would it take for us to find out? I knew Corvi went by every couple of weeks, but he didn't go upstairs; he used his mail key to open the mailbox on the ground floor and shove some cash into it. "If I ever go by and the cash is still there, then I'll know she's dead," he told me.

I didn't feel like playing the good daughter-in-law and insisting that we go visit her, the way my family had visited Abuela. I thought about it, but I didn't say anything. Corvi didn't need me to pretend to be a good daughter-in-law.

The phone rang one afternoon and when I picked it up I heard her voice, quavering. "Hello, is Corvi available? This is his mother. Moira Welliver," she added piteously."

"Moira? It's me, Analie."

"Oh, Anna Lee! I thought it might be you, but I wasn't sure! Is Corvi there, honey?"

"No, he's at work," I said. "Is something wrong...?"

"Yes. I really need to speak with Corvi. It's an emergency."

"Ummmm..." I considered this. "You want him to try and stop by after work? I think he might be leaving about now— I'm not sure. I could try and catch him."

"Would you, please, honey? Please?"

I dialed the precinct and amazingly, got Corvi on the phone.

"Hey, baby, I was just about to take off. Everything okay?"

"Your mom called and she sounded really upset."

"Oh, Christ. What's the problem?"

"I don't know, she didn't say..." I hesitated at this part. "She said she needs to talk to you, it's an emergency."

Corvi groaned.

"Fu——ck," he intoned, making the one-syllable word into something long and tortured. "All right, I'll stop by for five seconds and see what she wants and then I'm coming home. We'll order pizza?"

"Sure," I said.

But an hour went by, and then another, and then I got nervous and impulsively threw on a jacket and walked the two blocks to her apartment building. It was very much like Abuela's, but a little shabbier. Someone was coming out when I arrived, so I didn't buzz—I just went up. I hadn't been back since Corvi and I had left together that day, which seemed like so long ago. The hallway smelled like soup and there was a faint buzzing sound that accompanied the sound of my footsteps as I walked to Moira's door. When I pressed the buzzer, nothing happened, so I knocked. After about thirty seconds, I tried again, but harder.

I heard some rustling and mumbling, and then Corvi's voice yelling, "Yeah?"

"Corvi, it's me."

"Hold on, I'm coming." More rustling. I jumped when the lock snapped open from inside and the doorknob jiggled; then the door edged its way open and Corvi was standing there with an unlit cigarette hanging out of his mouth, looking exhausted. His hair stood a little bit on end, and his t-shirt was dirty. "Hey, baby."

"I just came over," I said unnecessarily. I was relieved to see him. "I got worried."

"That's nice." He opened the door a little more and stood back. "Come on in—if you can."

I stepped in, tentatively, and then drew in a sharp breath. I remembered the apartment as merely bleak and dusty, but it had been transformed now into a kind of hellish cave in which the stalagmite that rose up off the floor were made of stacks and stacks of newspapers and magazines, tied with string and piled on top of each other and collapsing onto other things. There were columns of folded clothes, dozens and dozens of paperback books, and housewares; a floor fan, an old vacuum cleaner, three tiny wooden chairs—like the kind I sat on in elementary school— and a row of ceramic lamp bases lined up like prisoners, their shadeless bulb sockets looking shamed. I could barely see the floor save for a shuddering path that made its way through the living room and then became a forked road leading to both the kitchen and Moira's bedroom in the back. The air was heavy and stifling and it smelled bad, like spoiled food.

"Corvi? Who is it?" I heard Moira's tremulous voice.

"It's Analie," snapped Corvi. He shook his head at me.

"What's happened?" I whispered.

"Well, she's lost her cat," said Corvi, pointedly raising his voice. "I didn't even know Mom had a cat, but she swears she does, and now she can't find it in—in all this."

"Oh, my God," I breathed.

"What's that? I can't fucking hear you," yelled Corvi over his shoulder. "Jesus," he said. "Come in. I guess. I'm a little worried for your safety. It's a fucking hazard."

I felt worried too. I took a few more steps in and Corvi shut the door behind me.

"When I got here, it was completely dark," he went on.

"Apparently Moira here has forgotten how to replace a light bulb. She has enough—in the kitchen I'd say there's, oh, about a hundred. But she doesn't know what to do with them."

I was finally able to see Moira, huddled on the couch in a bathrobe. A space had been cleared off so that she could sit and watch television. The TV set was bookended by more towering structures of magazines, and at its base were a collection of ragged teddy bears, as well as a blender still in the box and what looked like disassembled camping gear.

"Hi, honey," said Moira. "I'm sorry you have to see me like this. I'm a mess."

I was speechless. Moira's hair was completely gray and stood out around her head like an explosion. She looked very old.

"So, I got off work," said Corvi, continuing in an exaggeratedly aggrieved tone. "And I came here and I've spent the last fucking two hours here doing menial bullshit like changing lightbulbs and unclogging the filthiest fucking toilet I've ever seen. And I work in the ghetto, Mom." Corvi was standing with his arms folded, surveying the scene around him. "I hauled out like five bags of spoiled food, because for some reason Moira here had shit like, like, twenty packages of butter in a fridge that's been turned down to the temperature of a heated pool..."

"The price of butter keeps going up!" cried Moira.

"Well, you know how much melted, rotten butter is worth? Zero dollars," said Corvi. "Actually, less than that. In the negative, because of how much it stinks and what a fucking pain in the ass it is to dispose of it."

"I'm sorry. I told you I needed help."

"That's right," said Corvi. "That's why you gave me the old ring-a-ding-ding. Oh, and you know what else is in the kitchen, Analie? Bills and notices, like, wow. Mom, tell me something. Why the fuck am I busting my goddamn hump at work and dropping off money here every week if you ain't paying your fucking bills? Your rent?"

"I ran out of checks," said Moira piteously.

"You know what?" Corvi picked up a long, narrow painting of a bullfighter. He regarded it for a moment and then threw it onto the floor. Moira let out a shriek.

"That's worth something!" she screamed, but Corvi shook his head.

"You need to call your brother," he said to her coldly. "Phillip? He still in Philadelphia? Philadelphia Phillip? He's gotta come get you and take you with him, or put you into a home or something, 'cause clearly you're not fit to live among normal people who do shit like, I dunno, mop their fucking floors and take out the goddamn garbage."

"No, Corvi, no. Please." Moira was crying; tears ran down her cheeks, and she wiped her nose on the sleeve of her bathrobe. "I just need your help."

Corvi continued shaking his head. "What, with finding your cat? If it's still here it's dead, Mom. And of all the cat turds I seen around here, there haven't been any fresh ones. So, the budding detective inside me says either the cat took off or dropped dead. When Phillip comes and clears you out, I'm sure you'll find the remains and give them a proper burial." Moira cried harder. "What made you think you could take care of a cat? You were like, *Hmm, I failed as a mother, so let me try something else.* Well, guess what? You failed at taking care of a *cat.* A litter box was too much of a commitment for you? Couldn't buy cat food on the regular?" Corvi turned his attention to me. "You know, Analie, I could have used a litter box when I was a kid. June Cleaver here used to go beserko if I had an accident—which happened all the time. I was afraid to get out of bed at night, so I'd piss myself. And my mother here—and her special lady friend, Marilyn, when she was gracing us with her presence— wouldn't change the sheets or give me clean underwear. Hey, there's an idea," Corvi said, tapping his head. "Call up Marilyn and you can go live with her. Then you'll know what it's like to starve during the day and sleep in your own piss at night."

"Corvi, please."

"Please what?" Corvi stepped over a pile of *TV Guides* and was back at the door, gesturing for me to come with him. "If you choose Marilyn over Phillip, then just tell Marilyn you'll go to her. She isn't to set one foot in Gravesend. If she does, I swear to God I will cut her throat from ear to ear and bleed her out, and then I'll take her to the ghetto and set her body on fire, do you understand? Tell her that. I'm the police, I'll get away with it. And no one will fucking miss her. Or you, for that matter." He glanced over at me quickly and then looked away while Moira buried her face in her hands, sobbing. Then she raised her head and looked at me.

"Please, Anna Lee," she gulped between heaving breaths. "Tell him to help me. You liked me, didn't you? We had fun together when you stayed here. I opened my home to you, didn't I? I saved all these magazines so we could look at hair- styles together. I have *Cosmopolitan*."

I didn't say anything, and Corvi opened the door for me.

"Go ahead, baby," he said. "Goodbye, Mom. Good luck with everything. I'm sure the road ahead of you is paved with rainbows and daisies, if you can just find it in all this crap..."

I stared at Moira one last time before I turned and gingerly made my way to where Corvi was standing and waiting for me.

"The cat," she called after us. "It was Corvi, too." I couldn't see her anymore from where I was standing, I could only hear her voice. Corvi turned around, slowly.

"What did you say?"

"I named the cat Corvi," she said. "I missed calling for you, having you around."

He snorted at that.

"Well, Corvi's dead," he said. "Dead or gone. What's the difference?"

3.

Exactly one week after the police discovered the burning car, Corvi escorted me upstairs to the Barrett's apartment. "I'll say hi to Reese," he told me, and I nodded.

"Hey, man," Reese said, ignoring me and shaking hands with Corvi as enthusiastically as if they were frat brothers. "I'm glad you stopped by today. I actually just got a call from Detective Purcell. Sounds like he's finally taking all this seriously—"

I was removing Brook's bib, which was caked with oatmeal and pureed banana. I set it on the table and then lifted him out of his high chair. He wrapped his arms around my neck and I saw Corvi looking on with a proud, approving expression before he tore his eyes away from me and said, "I'm sorry, what?"

"They said they want me to come down and look at some security footage," repeated Reese obligingly. He raised his eyebrows, waiting for Corvi's reaction. I watched Corvi's face subtly register this comment with a fleeting expression of anxiety that Reese didn't seem to pick up on.

"Security footage?"

"Yeah. It took them a while, but they finally got in touch with the owner of the garage across the street from where the car was found. I guess there was also a language thing, the guy doesn't speak too much English. Anyway, he's been robbed a bunch of times so he set up a security camera. His nephew comes and puts in a new tape once a week and they label the old ones and put them aside. Purcell said he has, like, hundreds. Anyway, he and another officer went through them and found the footage of that day. He wants me to come in and see if I recognize the person on the tape."

"Wow," said Corvi. "They—they actually have someone on video?"

Reese made a face. "Well, that's the thing. Purcell said it's really hard to make out, but he wanted me to come in and see it anyway."

"Amazing," murmured Corvi. "Do you want me to give you a lift? I've got the car."

"Hey, man, that would be great," said Reese, slipping on his jacket. "I thought you took the subway into the city."

"I did when I was in the two-oh, but I've been transferred to Bed-Stuy. Makes more sense to drive."

"Bed-Stuy?" Reese looked impressed. "Isn't that like a— like a war zone or something?"

"You have no idea," said Corvi. He was patting his pockets, looking for cigarettes. "I'll take you out with me on a ride-along sometime if you want to have your mind blown."

"God, that'd be amazing," Reese said, his face lighting up. What an idiot. The first thing that came to my mind was Corvi pushing Reese out of the passenger side of the squad car while doing fifty miles an hour on the Brooklyn Queens Expressway. Reese gave Brook an absent-minded kiss on the head and said, "Thanks, Analie. I'm going into work later, so I'll see you this evening."

"Sure," I said tightly.

"Bye, baby," said Corvi. He shot me a significant look. "I love you."

I wanted nothing more than to wait around the apartment, hoping that Corvi would call me, but it was pointless. Everything having to do with the police took hours. I wasn't even sure if he'd have information to give me—for all I knew, he would drive Reese to the precinct and then take off. But I was hoping though that he'd be able to talk his way in to seeing the tape. I was dying to know what was on it.

I got Brook changed and dressed, wrangling his wriggly body into a shirt and pants, socks and shoes. We went to the playground and I trailed him as he toddled around. Sometimes I held out my hand and he grasped it when he needed help balancing. I said, "You're okay!" brightly every time he fell down, and scooped him up quickly, setting him on his feet before he had time to cry. I took a small Hot Wheels car out of my bag and handed it to him so he could run around holding it. I gave dirty looks to other children when they approached him, looking like they might try to take the car. I offered him snacks. Basically, it was the usual bubble we existed in, where Brook explored a tiny little slice of the world and I shadowed him, anticipating his needs and trying to balance that with giving him space. I tried not to look at my watch every five minutes. I daydreamed. And finally, I told him Brook it was time to go. I eased the transition with a box of raisins. He loved raisins.

I was steering the stroller toward the gate when I saw Reese standing there, waiting for us. My stomach lurched as I approached him.

"Hi...?" It trailed off into a question. *Hi? What are you doing here?*

"Hey, Analie," said Reese, hands in his pockets. "I was hoping I'd find you here. God, you make it look so easy, you know that? We're so lucky to have you. You're a natural. Even with all this stuff going on, life's like one big party for Brook. That's all you."

"Everything okay?" But I didn't really need to ask. Reese looked calm and he was smiling, although he wasn't showing his gums.

"Yeah, fine," he said. "I'm blowing off work... they showed me the tape at the precinct and then I just turned around and came back home." He bent over the stroller, reaching forward to touch Brook's face. "Hi, buddy." Then he turned back to me. "Where are you headed?"

"Just to your place," I said. "Now is when I usually bring Brook back for his nap."

"Can I join you?"

"Of course." We began to walk together down Seventh Avenue, taking our time. Reese was quiet. "How did it go?" I finally asked.

"It was—it was pretty much useless. Corvi came in with

me," he added. "It was nice of him. But there is nothing to see on that tape. It's grainy and gray and just—total shit. You see the car drive past, for what that's worth. About a half hour later, someone walks by but there's nothing to go on. It's just—a figure. Could be man, woman, old, young... There's a fence, and the tape is jumpy. So, you see someone enter the frame, but right away they're behind part of the fence. Then the tape jumps a little, and they're behind the next part of the fence. It's infuriating. Whoever it is, they're not running. Just—strolling. Calm as can be. And somehow ending up hidden at every step. Dumb luck."

"What do the police think?"

"They think it might be Mia. No one else walks by, at least in that direction."

"Could you tell at all? Anything?"

"I thought for sure I would know when I saw the tape—that I'd see something the detectives missed. How can you look at someone and not know if it's your wife?" He paused, the breeze ruffling his hair. "But I think—I think it's her. It has to be. There's no one else on the tape. Something about the—just the hint of the gait, it's—sort of feminine and—I think it's her and she's walking—" Reese snapped his fingers "—right out of our lives. Of Brook's life. It's crazy. Who would do that? I don't feel like I knew her at all. It's sick."

"I'm sorry, Reese," I said. I reached over and touched his arm. "I can't imagine how anyone could do that. To their family."

"Of course you can't," said Reese, looking at me fondly. "Hey, listen. Can I come back with you, and hang around today? Or will I be in the way?"

"That would be great," I said. "I mean, if you're sticking around, I can go home—"

"No," he said. "I want you to stay."

4.

The phone was ringing when I let myself into Abuela's apartment. Our apartment. I slammed the door shut and ran for it.

"Hello?"

"Analie, where the hell have you been?"

"Hey, Corvi. I'm sorry. I stayed to have pizza with Reese and Brook—"

"Jesus Christ, is he paying you for that? He better be fucking paying you."

I couldn't think of what to say. Although I barely looked at the crumpled bills Reese gave me at the end of each week, I was pretty sure he was not, in fact, paying me to have dinner with him and Brook. Usually when he got home, he asked me tentatively if I wanted to stay for dinner, and as long as Corvi was working, I said yes. It did not feel like dinner in any professional capacity. It felt like we were a family.

"Totally," I finally said. There was a lot of noise in the background. I could tell Corvi was calling from a payphone. "So, you saw the tape?"

"Yeah," he said. "I offered to go up with Reese, give him moral support. But there's nothing. You can't see who it is."

"That's what Reese said..."

"Oh, he told you already. You don't need to hear it from me."

"Corvi—"

"Okay, Analie. I'll see you—hold on," Corvi yelled suddenly. "Sorry, baby, I gotta go."

"Corvi," I said again desperately, and then we were disconnected.

I felt jumpy after that, and I decided to do laundry. It was a chore I always did in the household, just as Corvi wordlessly and without complaint hauled the garbage out on his way to work. I'd noticed he did it when he lived with Moira, too, just automatically detouring into the kitchen and tying up the trash and bringing it downstairs with them. No matter how horrible he was being to Moira, he still took the garbage out. And Mama had always done our laundry when I was growing up, a chore I then took over. I noticed Corvi and I had settled into the roles we'd grown up with, at least a little bit. It made me wonder if we were replaying the lifetimes we'd lived growing up, stepping in and out of being children, and maybe playing at being our parents? Each other's parents? No. I didn't believe that. We were nothing like the grownups who'd raised us. Corvi couldn't be more different than my parents, and I loved him, I took care of him, nothing like Moira. I knew I'd upset him on the phone, that he'd sensed the closeness between me and Reese, and I was sorry.

Doing the laundry was something that made me feel close to him, like I had when I'd stayed with him and Moira and washed and dried and folded his clothes. He didn't have a lot, but the items were all sensible, and innocent somehow. Thick gray sweatpants and sweatshirts, his white shorts, the blue precinct t-shirt that read *The Alamo Under Siege*. Two pairs of blue jeans. Sneakers. Dress shoes. His socks were new; I'd gotten rid of the old ones and gotten him white crew socks. He owned one suit and two police uniforms. One of them were the blues that he wore on his beat, and the other was formal attire for funerals and ceremonies.

The laundry room was empty when I went down to the basement, which was a relief. No neighbors, no small talk, no sidelong glances from the old people who remembered me as a little girl. I stuffed all the contents of our bag into one washer, since there wasn't anyone there to look at me disapprovingly and maybe even gesture to the sign that said *Do not overfill.* I placed my quarters in their allotted slots, and the detergent in the appropriate compartment. Then I sat and watched our belongings grudgingly turning around and around, hampered by overfilling, rising and falling laboriously amidst the suds. What would I do if the washer broke down because of me, and overflowed? Grab my stuff, I guess, and hightail it out of there so no one would know it was my fault. I thought about Reese and our pizza dinner, the way he watched me as I cut up Brook's pizza into tiny squares, adding some frozen peas to his plate to round out the meal. "Want some?" I joked, and Reese laughed and popped one in his mouth.

"Tastes like... ice," he said, shrugging.

"I hate peas," I told him, and he looked surprised.

"How can you hate peas, Analie? They're so cute."

"They are cute. But I don't like the way they taste. And they get so mushy."

"Oh, but you have to try fresh spring peas. Parboiled, at most. Crisp and fresh and—we'll get you some spring peas, Analie. They're going to turn your world upside down."

"Maybe," I said, sitting back down at the table. "So, my

Abuela used to make *arroz con pollo*, that was her big thing. And I loved it—except for the peas! I had to pick around them to get to the good stuff and I totally resented it. They were so in the way."

Reese laughed, with the gums. "What's—ar-roz—"

"*Arroz con pollo*. It's a big pot filled with chicken and rice and pieces of sausage and everything tastes so good, except for those—" I almost said *fucking*, and stopped myself "—those peas."

Brook took some of his food and threw it across the table, which made Reese laugh even harder.

"Watch what you say. Brook is going to end up resenting peas, too. And it'll be all your fault."

"I know, I'm a bad influence," I said, and Reese shook his head.

"God, you're anything but that," he said, still smiling.

I switched the clothes from the washer to two dryers and sat back down. The laundry room was windowless, painted white and gray, with two long tables. One was for folding clothes, and the other held assorted books and magazines that tenants left for people to look at. A lot of the books were Abuela's. After she and my parents had moved to Florida, I'd brought her books and magazines downstairs. All her *Ladies Home Journals*, and her romance novels.

"I don't know anything about your family," Reese said to me at dinner. "Your abuela, your mom and dad. You don't talk about them." I made a face and got up to clear the table, and he said, "You don't have to do that. Just sit and talk with me."

"I actually have to head home," I said, and Reese nodded and stood up.

"Of course. I'll let you go."

5.

My last phone conversation with my mother had been on a Sunday evening months before. It felt like centuries ago. Corvi, in just his shorts, sat on the couch dipping buttered toast into ketchup and telling me a work story that was terrible but made me laugh, too. It involved a rich older man who'd been wrapped in plastic cling wrap from head to toe by a male john. "Why?" I asked, giggling.

"Why, why, why?" he said, rolling his eyes. "Why do people do the things that they do?"

"But I mean, what was the purpose—"

"Oh, sexual gratification. It's always about that. Or money. In this case, both.""Gross," I said, laughing.

"Old guy's mother is still alive, too. Great to have to make that phone call. 'Uh, hello? I'm sorry to report that your son was fucking some male prostitute and decided he wanted to get all wrapped up like last night's leftovers...'"

I stopped laughing abruptly.

"Oh, shit," I said. "Dad wanted me to call tonight at six."

Corvi's face fell. "Oh, man. I'm sorry, baby. Look, why don't you skip it?"

"No, no. I'll do it," I said. But my spirits had crashed down to earth.

After a period of estrangement, my father asked that I call him and Mama on the first Sunday of every month at six o'clock. *Do it for your mother,* he said. I understood why, but I hated it. The conversations were awkward, painful. And yet, once a month, I made the call. My mother wanted it, and I didn't know how to say no. Or maybe I just felt like it was the least I could do. Mama and Dad were so thoroughly erased from my life, it was the only thing we had left to attest to the reality that yes, they were my parents. Yes, I was their daughter. This was all written in invisible ink, and our monthly phone call was like holding a flame to that ink and making it appear, however briefly.

That evening, I dragged myself to the phone and stood, slumped over, listening to it ring.

"Hello?" Mom's voice was querulous, suspicious, even though she knew it was me.

"Hi, Mama."

"Hola, Analie," she said coldly. "It's late. I didn't know if you were going to call."

I glanced at my watch; it was three minutes past six.

"*Como estás*, Mama? How's Dad?"

"Oh, you know," said Mama. "It's been raining a lot, and your papa has to have some new dental implants put in."

"How's Abuela?"

"The same. Ever since we got here, it's been downhill. You know she can't do anything for herself—"

"*Sí, yo se*," I murmured.

"We have to do everything for her, feed her, walk her to the toilet—" Mama said this every time we spoke. "Your father left her alone in her room yesterday because she was taking a nap. She fell out of the bed and stayed like that on the floor for an *hour*."

"I'm so sorry," I said.

A long, awkward silence. The line crackled a little bit.

"We have a new neighbor," Mama said grudgingly. "He

came by tonight and ate dinner with us. He's all alone in the world. His wife and daughter died in a car accident."

"That's terrible," I said dutifully.

"But I told him—well, God has a plan. Maybe He is trying to spare you the heartbreak your family can bring you later on."

"Mama!" I shrieked. Corvi, on the couch, craned his neck around to see what was going on. "Did you really say that?"

"Yes, I did," she said, sounding smug. "I said with the pain a daughter can bring you, sometimes it's good if they depart this world early. She's waiting for you in a better place, we know that for sure. And your heart's broken now, but she can't cause you no more pain in your life."

"That is so—*estúpido*, Mama!"

"Watch your mouth please, Analie. Maybe this is the way you talk to people now—"

"Why don't you ask me how I'm doing? And Corvi? He's my husband—"

"Don't say his name!" snapped my mother.

"I can't change what happened, Mama," I said helplessly. "These phone calls are always the same. Why don't you call *me* next month? I have to listen to this shit and pay the phone bill, besides?" I slammed down the phone. Corvi hopped over the side of the couch and was kneeling in front of me, telling me he was sorry that my parents were such assholes, that I had him and it was all I needed. At the time, it made me feel better, but now I thought of what Reese would say. He would never call my parents assholes. He would probably want to visit them in Florida, take Brooky with us, do some emotional healing. And of course, my parents would love them both. I could imagine my mother

165

and father admiring Reese's hearty, wholesome good looks, and Brook's baby beauty.

Ay, he has the face of an angel, my mother would murmur, her voice soft and warm, not like the stranger I heard on the phone. *And you're so good with him, Analie. He loves you.*

6.

I was restless, I couldn't sit around and wait for the clothes to finish drying, so I went back upstairs to the apartment and roamed around. It wasn't very late, but it was dark outside and the world around me seemed to be asleep. I looked out the window where, so many years before, I'd seen Tenny standing outside in her cut-off shorts and old-fashioned shirt. I had a sudden, chilling feeling that she'd be standing there again, this time awash in the orange light of the streetlights. But there was no one. I pictured Reese there instead, looking up at me, throwing pebbles against the window glass, and then I saw Corvi stride into the frame of my vision with a gun pointed directly at Reese's head. I shook my head and went back downstairs. I was pulling the hot clothes out of the dryer when a massive wad of bills fell from the folds of Corvi's jeans, onto the floor. I picked them up, wondering how much it was, and was startled when I peeled away one five-dollar bill only to find another, and then a clump of ones, and then more fives, like a magic trick, until I counted a hundred dollars. I stared at the warm, wrinkled money, and then uncertainly put it into my pocket. This had to be from some type of bet Corvi had made at work, in the locker room, maybe over a beer. When I got upstairs, I dumped the clothes onto the bed and placed the bills on top of the dresser, smoothing them out as best I could. Then I got to work folding, but I was already tired of the laundry. As soon I finished stuffing the last shirt into a drawer, I climbed out of my jeans and crawled onto the bed in just a t-shirt and underwear.

The room was warm. I lay on top of the bedspread and listened to the familiar sounds of Gravesend outside. I was really waiting for Corvi to come home, waiting for his key in the lock, but it was close to morning and I was sound asleep when he got back. I only woke when I heard him emptying his pockets, placing coins on top of the dresser, the soft rustling sound as he took his shirt off. I kept my eyes closed and listened as he paused, then took hold of the crumpled bills I'd left for him. It was a subtle sound—the crinkling of money in a weary palm. He unzipped his jeans and stepped out of them, sighing. I was sure he'd get into bed, but instead he left, closing the door softly behind him.

I got up and went into the living room. Corvi was sitting on the couch, using his thumb and forefinger to rub at the bridge of his nose. In his other hand he still held the wad of bills.

"Hey," I said. I sat down beside him.

"Hey."

"I found all that money while I was doing the laundry."

"Ohhhh, it went through the wash," he said. His eyes were closed and his voice was sleepy. "That's why it doesn't stink anymore."

"What?"

"Their money. It stinks. Just like they do. Their apartments. The second you walk in the door—before, even. Just climbing up the stairs. And then even after I leave, it's stuck in my nostrils. I could swear it's on my blues."

Tentatively, I reached a hand over and let it rest on his hair.

"Who are you talking about?"

"Who do you think? The skels. The citizens I serve and protect...We go in there... we break shit up... we smack 'em around... and we take their stuff. I've taken money out of a dead man's pockets. What's he gonna do, file a report from the morgue? But that's easy. The old lady who calls us because her son's a junkie and he's robbed her blind—that's a little harder. We find the guy, take the money off him, split his face wide open, and tell him not to steal from his mommy. Then we go back to the old lady. 'Sorry, ma'am, he didn't have anything on him. Must have spent it on drugs.' What the fuck, the money was already stolen, right? Only difference is that now it's in our pockets instead of that junkie's. You know what me and Duffy gotta do when we go into one of those apartments? Keep moving, don't touch the walls or the furniture. Otherwise, we'll walk out with roaches in our blues, in our hair. Guy in the locker room the other day goes to undress and he's got cockroaches comin' outta his sleeve... The skels don't care, though. They're sittin' and loungin' around with a sea of rats and roaches all around them. The floors are practically moving by them-selves, and they've got their kids sitting in the middle of it, gettin' bitten up. If they're lucky. I went on a call where I had to kick in the door and the first thing these scum of the earth start saying when we bust in on them is 'It's her fault!' 'No, it's his fault!' They're blaming each other and pointin' fingers and you know what's in the bathroom? A dead kid. They got a starved, emaciated, beaten-up little kid, maybe just a little older than Brook Barrett, dead in the bathtub and the first thing they can think to do when they see me is start throwin' each other under the bus.

"You have no idea what I've seen," he finished, and he finally opened his eyes.

I was quiet for a moment and then I said, "No, I don't."

"But you see it in me, don't you? And you don't like it. Not anymore. You look at Barrett and see—what?" I shook my head, confused, and he sat up suddenly, bracing an arm across me so that I couldn't move. "The good life? Everything beautiful and clean? A ready-made family, maybe a suburban house with a backyard?"

"Oh, stop it."

"No, I get it. You see *possibility*. And you think his bull-shit's gonna rub off on you. It can't happen, Analie. Not for either of us. We're the burning class, remember? That never changes."

For a moment, I felt the rush of wind in my hair, Corvi's arm around me, the tart taste of a lollipop in my mouth.

Ricky's voice.

Well, now, I see this is where the high-class folk live.

And Corvi.

Yeah, well, fuck them. Here comes the burning class.

I was surprised he remembered that.

What had I felt right then, that night, when he'd said it?

Proud.

Happy to be part of who they were, what they were doing.

It was what I deserved, where I belonged.

Wasn't it?

That never changes.

"Shut up," I snapped suddenly, and I struggled to get away from him. Corvi grabbed me hard by both arms, leaning so close that we both tipped over and landed on the floor. It was so ungainly, it almost made me laugh. He stood first and then extended a hand, helping me up. His expression was both stone-faced and pained as we faced each other.

"I'm doing everything I do for us," he said slowly. "I am paying that witch doctor for how he helped us. Helped *you.* Tenny wasn't bothering me."

"What? Tenny was *my* demonic apparition? I'm sorry, I thought she was making both of us uncomfortable, but I guess it was just me."

"Why are you being such a bitch?" Corvi seemed genuinely bewildered. "Fuck this, I need coffee." He pushed past me and went into the kitchen, and I followed him.

He gave me a sidelong glance as he filled the teakettle with water and slammed it down on the stove. *Tick-tick-tick-tick* when he turned on the gas, and then *whoosh.*

"I didn't say it right," he said. "Of course Tenny bothered me. I've never seen anything like it. She gave me nightmares. I'm still not totally convinced that she wasn't a bad dream. I just meant—I meant that I did this for you. For us."

"What did you do, exactly?"

Corvi threw his head back, staring at the ceiling, and groaned.

"What did I *do*? I'm still doing it, baby! I'm working my fucking tail off!"

"Do you want me to talk to Adán? Maybe he can, like, give us a break."

Bracing himself against the sink, Corvi now looked down at the floor, shaking his head. I folded my arms across my chest and looked out the window.

"She liked you, you know," I said. "Tenny. She had a crush on you."

"Okaaaaay..."

"Do you really not remember? We used to call your house when we were kids, and prank you."

"*You* did?"

"Me and Tenny. She looked up your number in the phone book. Sometimes we just hung up when you answered, but I talked to you—" He looked astonished. "I told you that someone liked you, and you asked if it was the girl who looked like a corpse. You and your friends called her the dead girl."

"You called me and we *talked*?" Corvi had a little smile on his face, as though I were relaying a romantic anecdote. "Why didn't you ever tell me?"

"Do you remember?"

He rubbed his head. "I don't, baby, I'm sorry. I mean, I remember that we called her the dead girl. Wow. We spoke on the phone, all those years ago?"

"Yes," I said impatiently. "That's not the point, though. The point is that you talked about Tenny in a terrible way, and she was listening the whole time. She was crushed. And not just that time. You treated her like garbage whenever you saw her. You were making fun of her."

Corvi spread his hands out. "So? I mean, really—so what?"

"She wasn't just *my* ghost, Corvi. I'd say she had a bone

to pick with both of us. So don't go acting like you did me this huge favor."

"I swear to God, Analie. I have no idea where you're going with this. Fine, I wanted to get rid of her, too. For us. I wanted us to move on."

"Move on to what?"

"Well, I want to..." Corvi rubbed the back of his head, suddenly smiling shyly. "Like, to start a family."

"*What?*"

"I want us to have a baby," he said. His smile disappeared when he saw my expression. "Oh wow, you don't like that idea, do you?"

"Why?"

"Why? Why what?"

"Why do you want to have a baby with me?"

"You don't think—you don't think you already have a baby, do you?" Corvi's eyes widened. "Brook isn't *yours*, Analie. You can't just take something that doesn't belong to you like that."

"Brook needs me," I said. "I'm a huge part of his life."

"And Barrett? Does he need you, too?"

I didn't know what to say. I wanted to yell, *Yes, he needs me. They both need me.* But I couldn't bring myself to say it out loud. I didn't need to, though. Corvi heard me anyway.

"*Goddamnit, Analie.*" The coffee cup in his hand fell to the floor and broke into pieces. Corvi drove a fist into the wall so hard that a piece of plaster peeled away right in front of us and fell off. I took a step backward and he grabbed me by the arms and stuck his face right into mine. "Being around Barrett doesn't make you good, Analie. It doesn't clean you off. He doesn't know you. I know you. And I love you. Do you need me to tell him that you're not who he thinks you are? That me and you, we are two peas in a fucking pod? I'll be glad to tell him myself, how you have never once, and I mean *never*, shown any remorse for what happened that night. That it was your idea to set your own fucking family's house on fire. You lit the rockets! You didn't flinch when the place went up. As a matter of fact, the next thing I knew, your hand was down my pants in a cemetery—"

"Stop," I said desperately. Despite all that had happened that night, I didn't want him to make our story ugly.

But he kept going.

"I never saw you shed a goddamn tear for your parents, their house and all their belongings, or your friend who was stuck upstairs and burned to death—all because of you. Jesus Christ, no wonder she haunted you! Maybe I was a dick to her when we were kids, but I was just some neighborhood jackass. You were her friend, Analie!"

"Stop, please," I said weakly.

"You have no idea what I've done for you," Corvi said, his face inches from mine. His eyes looked wet, suddenly, and to my astonishment, his chin quivered and he began to cry. He let go of me and rubbed at his eyes. "I'm getting the money so I can pay Adán. For us. I just want you to know how I'm doing it. By taking money off drug dealers and junkies and even old ladies, sometimes. By patting down corpses. By wading through shit and breathing in that smell. By beating the crap out of people, jackin' 'em up until I hear their bones breaking. So the least you could do for me, Analie, is have a fucking baby with me so we can be a family. And stop looking at Reese Barrett like he's the gold standard of purity and goodness. Trust me, he's *fucked*, just like everyone else."

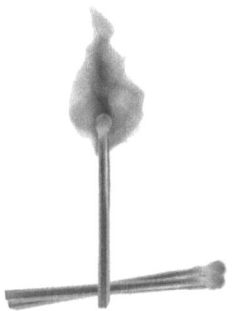

VIII.
A History Of Fire

1.

Reese called me first thing in the morning, just as I was getting out of the shower. I heard Corvi pick up the phone with a tight "Welliver." Then he paused and said, "Hey, man." I stepped into the room, wrapped in a towel, and Corvi handed me the phone. "It's Barrett," he said. He stared at me briefly and then pointedly walked out of the room. That was for show—I was certain he would be eavesdropping from wherever in the apartment he was.

"Hi, Reese," I said. "Everything okay?"

"Hey, Analie. I'm so sorry, I screwed up. I forgot that Brook has a doctor's appointment this morning. It's just his checkup, but—well, we'll be back around noon at the latest, I'd say. I'm so sorry. I forgot. Do you mind coming in late? I feel awful, you're probably up and getting ready when you could have been sleeping in..."

"Sure, no problem," I said. I re-wrapped the towel around my body, tucking in one corner so that it would stay put. "Noon?"

"Yeah, I can't imagine we'll be any later than that. Hey, we could, uh, have lunch before I go to work. I'll pick up some fixings."

"That sounds really nice," I said. My voice had gotten soft, and I quickly adjusted it to sound more professional. "Okay, I'll see you then."

2.

As I got closer to the Barretts, I made resolutions. I wasn't going to allow myself to get closer to Reese, I wasn't going to get wrapped up in any of his smiles—the creamy close-mouthed one, or the vulnerable one that showed his gums.

But Reese wasn't smiling at all when he let me in.

"Hey, Analie," he said.

I felt my own smile falter. "Are you okay?"

"Yeah," he said. He led me into the living room, where Brook was sitting and playing with those blocks again—stacking them up, knocking them over.

"Is there—is there news?"

"No, no. We just—well, we went to the doctor—"

"For the checkup. Is Brook all right?"

"Well, he's healthy, and he's big enough," said Reese. "He's using his fingers to eat, and so on. But the pediatrician is a little concerned..."

"About what?"

"Well, about the fact that Brook isn't hitting his speech

milestones. She was worried. He doesn't talk—at all. No babbling. No da-da, ma-ma, uppy..."

"All babies do stuff at different times—"

"That's what I said. But she's concerned. She asked if he responds to his name or little commands, you know, like 'Bring the ball to Daddy' kind of thing. She wondered if maybe he's internalizing the trauma of what's happened..."

"No, no," I said hurriedly. "He's fine. Look at him."

We looked. Brook wasn't stacking more than three blocks at a time. Feeling our eyes on him, he stared back at us. It was a little strange that he didn't talk at all. Corvi had noticed it too. "Does the kid ever say a word?" he'd asked, and I'd felt defensive and said *Sure, he makes sounds and he babbles and everything.* But the truth was he really didn't.

Still staring back at us, Brook bunched up his lips, turned red, and started to cry.

"Did he eat?" I asked, as I quickly scooped him up. It was his nap time, but I usually only put him down after lunch.

"I let him have a McDonald's burger," whispered Reese in the same ashamed way he might have admitted to giving Brook a shot of tequila. I was surprised, though. Reese, who didn't eat meat. Reese, who was so quick to talk about animal cruelty. He looked near tears himself.

"It's fine," I assured him, and then I took Brook into his room. I placed him, sobbing, on the changing table and pulled off his soft gray pants. There was a Band-Aid stuck to one chubby thigh where he'd apparently had blood drawn or received a vaccination of some kind. His diaper was dry. I wondered if he'd had anything to drink. As I doused his bottom with baby powder, he calmed down and just stared at me, as if he knew that sleep was coming. His nap, his routine. Reese taking him to the doctor had thrown him off. Sure enough, after I put on a fresh diaper and rocked him, he was very quiet and still, and I placed him carefully on his back in the crib, then pulled the slats up.

Reese was standing in the living room by the couch when I came back.

"He was just tired," I said.

"You're so wonderful with him, Analie," said Reese. "I don't know what we would do without you. I think—I think all this stuff with Mia being gone has messed him up. It's been traumatic and I—I haven't been able to give him what he needs. I've tried. Trust me. I'd do anything for him. But I've failed. I let him down."

"Reese, no," I said. "Are you kidding me? You're an amazing father. You were before—before Mia—before she was gone. And you are now. That hasn't changed."

Reese was rubbing the back of his neck, shaking his head. "But I haven't been able to give him something he needs. God, what happened to us? We were fine, we were a happy family—I thought. It's like something infected us, like a—a sickness. I'd love to blame it on his mother, for apparently taking off and leaving us. But I should have been able to fill in the blanks. I should have seen someone, asked for help. I'm the adult, it's my job to help him through it... he can't express himself..."

I put my hands up against his chest, I wanted to comfort him, and then suddenly he was putting his hands on either side of my face, just like he had that time in the kitchen, and kissing me. I gave in to the kiss, I didn't hold back. He was a surprisingly passionate kisser. Somehow, I'd never imagined him using his tongue so much, but he did, and he eased down onto the couch, pulling me with him. *Analie, Analie,* he murmured in between kisses. *God, I'm sorry. I know this is wrong. But I'm in love with you, Analie. I'm in love with you.* I could have listened to him say it a hundred more times. I'd always been intrigued by that manly chest, the hair peeking out of his button-down shirts when he left the first top buttons undone. The shirt he was wearing was white, with thin stripes of blue, open to a V and exposing the thick, dusky hair. He watched me unbutton it, his chest heaving. I stole a look up at him and saw that he was very serious. He wasn't going to be funny or talk dirty to me, like Corvi. I stopped thinking about Corvi as Reese put his big hands under my shirt, moaning again as his palms spanned my bare flesh over my ribcage. *Oh, God, you feel so good*, he said, just like he had in my daydreams. I hesitated for a moment because I was almost worried that his virtue would surface and he'd stop what was happening, but then I let go of him and pulled my shirt off. *Oh, God, Analie,* he said again. *You're so beautiful, oh, my God*, and he surprised me again, pulling my bra down and burying his face in my chest.

The buzzer rang.

We froze and looked at each other, and Reese said, "You've gotta be kidding me."

"What should we do?"

"Wait," said Reese. "Maybe it's a package, or someone rang the wrong apartment."

We waited. The buzzer rang again.

"Shit," said Reese. I eased off of him and he got up, pulling at the crotch of his pants and wincing. At the intercom, he stabbed viciously at the talk button and said, "Hello?"

"Mr. Barrett?" As usual, the connection was loud and yet somehow barely audible. "This is Detectives Purcell and Massey."

Reese laughed despite himself and shook his head as he pressed the buzzer, allowing the detectives entry into the building.

"They're like the goddamn make-out police," he said wryly, and I giggled.

Staring at me, he buttoned his shirt back up, but not before I saw that the hair was exclusive to his upper chest; his bare stomach was smooth. I was sick with the idea that our undressing was going in reverse, that I wasn't going to have his body, and give him mine. I stood and slipped on my shirt, smoothing out my hair. Reese smoothed out his, too, but it was still tousled. My mouth felt swollen from those kisses.

Reese opened the door as soon as he heard them approaching.

"The baby's sleeping," he said by way of greeting.

"Sorry we rang the buzzer, I hope it didn't disturb him," said Purcell in a way that somehow communicated that he didn't give a shit. "We'll be very quiet." He and Massey entered, nodding at me, and Reese quietly closed the door behind them. As usual, the detectives were both wearing suits. Purcell's tie was a muted shade of maroon, and Massey's was bright yellow. I wondered if the ties were their version of good cop, bad cop.

"What's going on?"

"Miss Welliver, I'm glad you're here," said Purcell in a low voice. "We actually wanted to speak to both of you."

I folded my arms across my chest and tried to look like a

normal, innocent nanny. No history of fire, no death, no making out with her employer.

"Mr. Barrett," started Purcell. He frowned and then went on. "Are you usually at home when you have a nanny to watch the child?"

"No," said Reese snappishly. "I took him for a checkup this morning, and Analie's just arrived."

"Okay," said Purcell, shrugging. "So—we've recently been made aware of some information—"

"About Mia?"

"Well, tertiary to the case," said Massey. I wondered if he knew what the hell he was saying, and I shifted my weight impatiently from one foot to the other.

"Mr. Barrett, are you aware that Miss Welliver here has been connected to arson, in the past?"

My mouth opened in surprise as Reese said, "Wait— what?"

"What do you mean?" I jumped in. "I don't have any *connection*. It wasn't my fault."

Purcell held his hand up.

"What happened?" asked Reese.

"What we mean to say," interjected Massey. "Is that a few years ago, Miss Welliver's family home burned down in Windsor Terrace. Has she told you about that?"

"No," said Reese wonderingly. "It burned down—how?"

He directed the question to me, but Purcell answered. "Well, that's the thing. It was suspected arson, but they never caught anyone for it. In fact, that night in Gravesend and Park Slope, there were several cases of willful and malicious destruction of property by use of fire and pyrotechnic devices. But her parents thought—"

"No, they didn't!" I said, frantically.

Massey shrugged and went on.

"—At the scene and later on during an interview, her parents expressed concern that Miss Welliver and her boyfriend at the time—that would be Officer Corvi Welliver —had something to do with the fire."

"They didn't really think that," I said. "And—I mean, it could have been a cigarette or a candle—"

"No, it was pretty clear someone basically blew the house up," said Massey.

"Who would do something like that?" Reese's face was pale.

"So Miss Welliver hasn't discussed this with you," stated Purcell flatly, and Reese shook his head in that same shocked, wondering way. "She hasn't told you that there was someone in the house at the time, a childhood friend—"

"Stop," I said. "Why are you telling him about it? It's horrible and it has nothing to do with Mia. Why are you stirring up shit like this?"

"You mean someone *died*?" Reese had gone from pale to a deathly white.

"Yes," said Purcell, and both he and Massey nodded with what seemed like exaggerated solemnity. "Both Miss Welliver and her parents were out at the time, but there was a childhood friend who was waiting for Miss Welliver to return home."

"Which I didn't know," I said, and then felt very conspicuous. "Who told you all this?"

"We're not at liberty to say," said Massey with a sidelong glance at Purcell.

"Oh, come on."

"It was an anonymous tip," said Purcell.

Now Reese scrunched up his face in confusion.

"You mean someone called and told you?"

"Yes," said Purcell again. "Someone phoned us anonymously and suggested that we look into Miss Welliver's past with regards to destruction of property by fire, which happened to include someone's car. Granted, nothing was ever linked to Miss Welliver or Officer Welliver, and no charges were filed. It just seemed like a—"

"Like a strange coincidence," finished Massey.

Reese looked at me. "Analie?"

"Oh, my God, this is such bullshit," I snapped, still speaking in a hushed tone so as not to disturb Brook. "I'm sorry you have absolutely no leads about what's going on, but to bring up something like this—yes, my family home was burned to the ground and we lost everything. I don't know how it happened. I didn't know there were other fires that night until you said it just now. So now because you found Mia's—Mia's car burned up, this is the connection you're making? That someone burned my house down, and someone set fire to Mia's car, so it has to be related? And, by the way, my parents never—they never actually thought that I had anything to do with it." I almost said "Or Corvi" but at the last second decided to leave his name out of it. Maybe if they looked at him as the potential arsonist, it wouldn't be the worst thing. "They were all freaked out and emotional and hysterical, and they didn't like Corvi—"

"Okay," said Massey, raising his hand. "Well, we just wanted to run it by you and see if you'd mentioned it to Mr. Barrett."

"I didn't," I said sullenly. "I don't like to talk about it. You can imagine."

"Did you go to the girl's funeral?"

I hated him for asking.

"No," I said. "I couldn't. I was—I was crushed by the whole thing."

"Just one more quick question for now," said Purcell. "You didn't speak to your parents for a while after the fire—"

"There was so much happening, we were all in shock," I said.

"And can I ask, did you ever, uh, mend your fences with them, so to speak? You on good terms with them now?"

"They moved to Florida," I said. "But yes. We speak on the phone regularly." I held his gaze defiantly, and thought I saw a little smile tugging at the corners of his mouth as though he knew how terribly my last conversation with Mama and Dad had gone, months ago.

"All right," said Massey. "Well, we'll be in touch."

"Thank you for your time, Mr. Barrett. Miss Welliver." Purcell nodded at us and then tried the lock on the door. "How the hell do you unlock this thing?"

"Bottom lock," said Reese faintly. "Ah, got it," said Purcell. "Thanks again." Massey made a point of closing the door very quietly, with a significant look toward the back rooms.

"Reese," I said immediately. He was rubbing the back of his neck again.

"You never told me," he said.

"This is—I don't know why they—I'm sorry I never told you about what happened to me—to my family's house," I said desperately. "I never talk about it. It's true, it got burned down. I don't know how, or why, or what happened. Corvi and I were on our first date, actually. I don't know if the oven sparked, or—or what. We lost everything, and my parents never got over it. They moved down to Florida with Abuela and she had a series of strokes. I don't—I don't talk about it, ever. If I thought it had something to do with Mia, with what's going on, I would have said something. I swear. It never—the connection didn't occur to me."

"Who was the person who died?"

"This—this girl I'd been friends with when I was a kid. When we were younger she used to sneak through my bedroom window. Sometimes I was out and I'd—I'd come home and she was just sitting there on the bed. I guess that night she—she stopped by. We didn't know about it until the firefighters found her body."

"How awful," said Reese. "I'm so sorry."

"It's okay," I said, and then I corrected myself. "I mean, it's not, but—but it has nothing to do with—"

"Of course it doesn't," said Reese, shaking his head. "They are really—they're really grasping at straws here. If these are the people who are in charge of maintaining law and order in this city, we are in serious trouble." He gave me a weak smile. But I could tell he wasn't looking at me the same way. Something was different—the story had sullied me in his eyes. "Listen, I'd better—I'd better get to work. I never made us lunch like I said I would. I'm sorry."

"It's fine."

"Analie," began Reese, and then he stepped closer to me, putting his hand on the back of my head, drawing me in for a restrained, almost chaste kiss. "We'll talk more later, okay?"

3.

I got home hoping, desperately, that Corvi would be there, even after our awful conversation. He wasn't. I wasted time. I took a shower. I did a few dishes. Finally, I called the precinct and asked for him.

"Hi honey," said Shirley, the extremely old receptionist. She always said she was going to run off with Corvi and leave me "an old maid." She told me cheerfully that Corvi wasn't in that day and then—I felt her poking, subtly, at our private life—asked if everything was okay. I said yes and hung up. I walked around and around the apartment and I murmured Corvi's name. I was trying to figure something out, but I couldn't put my finger on it. In the bedroom, the top of the dresser was strangely empty.

The money.

Where was all that money?

I opened one drawer after another—nothing. I went into the living room and surveyed the entire space. Of course, Corvi could have hidden the money somewhere else, but I knew he hadn't. So that meant he'd taken it somewhere, given it to someone, disposed of it somehow.

Shit.

I tripped over my own legs trying to get out of the apartment as quickly as I could. Elevator, elevator, fuck, move, move, okay, taking the stairs. Two at a time. Sidewalk, feet pounding, pavement, pain in my ankles. People stared at me, but I didn't care, just keep going, walking, running, squinting in the sunlight, go, go, go. I felt like I was going to throw up by the time I got to Adán's storefront, sticky mucus plastered to my lungs and throat, and I was panting as I leaned heavily against the stoop, trying to catch my breath for just a moment, and then pushing myself forward again, opening the door of his office without knocking and—

There they were.

Corvi, Adán, and a young man with black eyes. They all stared at me with eyes wide, their faces solemn, except for Adán, who smiled. He wasn't surprised to see me, and he looked almost approving, like he'd underestimated me but was now slightly impressed. His desk was covered with Corvi's money, so much of it that it had spilled onto the floor and was at their feet. All that money. Who wouldn't do everything they could for that much money?

"Don't—" I started to choke the words out but Adán said, "Get her." The man with the black eyes pounced on me like a cat and we both fell to the floor. He rolled me onto my back and pinned my arms down.

"Corvi," I screamed. "I need to talk to you!"

"Hey, be careful!" Corvi yelled.

I struggled, arching my back, and a wet cloth was pressed firmly against my face.

"It's okay, Analie, it's gonna be okay," Corvi was murmuring.

Sweet, thick smell.

Good at first, and then terrible.

Plants. Life. Flowers. Fire. Death.

I opened my mouth to scream but I just got more of that smell inside me, filling me up. It was going to come spilling out at any moment, or I'd choke on it.

"Give it another moment," I heard Adán say, and then that was it. I was gone.

VI.
Welcome Back

I only slept over at Tenny's a few times before my mother put a stop to my visits. For all my bravado around Tenny—the way I boldly approached her to make friends, the fact that I always had candy money, my shining hair, my two attentive parents—there were times when I was deeply frightened.

Of Uncle Gene. The things that happened at 3AM. Maybe life itself.

Tenny knew I was afraid, even if she didn't know why.

At night, I was vulnerable to the world and every future inevitability: growing up, the human body, sex, responsibility, adulthood, death... the possibility of accidents, hospital stays, bad luck, strange conditions... natural disasters, weather damage, and even fires. Fire crossed my mind back then. I knew how damaging it was. It ripped through everything in its path, it was merciless and it was devastating. It was excruciating.

Tenny was very kind to me when I was afraid, and I

remember two particular times she tried to soothe me, having picked up on my unspoken anxiety. The first time, we were lying in bed and I felt myself beginning to cry and panic, and Tenny told me that in the morning, she would wake up before me and tape crepe paper to the ceiling fan, and then I could turn it on when I woke up and we could watch the crepe paper go around and around. The idea made me giggle and the giggling broke that terrible night spell. The second time was also at night. She offered to make me something called *matzo brie*. I declined, but I never forgot the musing tone to her voice as she tried to figure out how she could make me feel better, and the scratchy sound of her voice in the dark: "I can make you *matzo brie*." I whispered, *No thank you*, but maybe there was a part of me, a little part, that felt a tiny bit less anxious, because I fell asleep soon after that.

I woke up with Corvi's face directly over mine, grinning.

"What's going on?" I croaked. My mouth was dry.

"Welcome back," he said. He began to lower himself gently on top of me, but I squirmed out from under him.

'What's going on?" I said again, loudly this time. I was in my underwear, and I pulled the blankets up against my chest, feeling exposed.

"Hey, hey, hey," said Corvi, putting his hands up. "Everything's okay. You were asleep for a while, that's all. I was a little worried, honestly. I'm glad to see you awake even if you are still mad at me." I stared at him, trying to put my memories together into something that might feel like understanding. "You've been out of it for almost a week," Corvi said, propping himself up and regarding me fondly. His mood seemed warm, and he was more relaxed than I'd seen him for months.

"*What?*"

"I know, crazy, right?"

"That's impossible."

"You don't remember anything, huh? Yeah, you've been kinda like in a dream state or something. I helped you go to the bathroom to pee," he added, looking pleased with himself.

"After—after I went to Adán's?"

Corvi looked down and played with his wedding ring. "Well, yeah."

I rolled away from him and swung my legs over the side of the bed, standing up and pretending I wasn't dizzy at the suddenness of it. "Where're you going?" Corvi asked, surprised.

"What did the two of you do?"

Corvi got up out of bed and came towards me, with his hands up in the air again.

"Hey, Analie, come on."

"Fuck you," I yelled at him.

"Hey, hey, hey," he said again. "We helped you that first time, right? This was, we had to—we did this to help."

"To help *who?*"

"To help *us*, Analie. We were falling apart. I can't lose you."

"You and Adán *can go fuck yourselves.*" My voice rose and I was screaming it at the top of my lungs. I was thinking of Reese, of Brook. How had they managed without me all week? I looked around wildly and grabbed the first thing I could lay my hands on, an old jewelry box, and I threw it at

Corvi as hard as I could. He ducked his head and held his arms up as the jewelry box hit the bed and bounced, scattering tiny drawers and various chains and rings and knickknacks all over the floor. I threw everything else I could get my hands on, although some of it was almost comically ineffectual, like a blouse that drifted lazily to the floor. A glass paperweight with a flower trapped inside of it for eternity had more heft, and Corvi let out a yelp when it hit him on the shoulder. "It's over, Corvi. I'm done." I whipped around to get my clothes out of the dresser, but I felt Corvi's arm around my waist and suddenly I was whirled toward the bed and thrown down with a *whomp*. I twisted around and began to sit up, but Corvi was in front of me, gripping my wrists and pushing me backwards until he was on top of me, looking down, unsmiling and breathing heavily.

"You are done," he said softly, his hands still on my wrists, which he pinned against the bed. "You're done with Reese and Brook and all that bullshit and you're back to being mine and only mine, and we're gonna have a baby in nine months and be a family. *Entiendes?* So, you need to calm the fuck down, Analie. It's over."

My entire body was flooded with a sharp, icy fear.

"What are you talking about?" I whispered, hating how weak my voice sounded now, how afraid.

"Which part don't you understand? Do I need to say it again? We're having a baby."

Surely, I would know if I was pregnant before he did? When was the last time we'd even had sex?

"That's impossible, Corvi."

"Anything is possible," said Corvi softly. "There's no point in arguing with me. The deed is done, Adán says we are 100%." He cocked his head at me. "Don't worry, he stayed in his lane. The potions and all that crap, you know. But I did my part." He winked. "In fact, we gotta be careful. All this yelling and fighting and rolling around isn't good for the baby." My mouth was open. "It's too early to go to the doctor but we'll wait a few weeks and head on over so that we make sure to do everything right. All the right foods and lots of rest, and no smoking or drinking just to be on the safe side. I'm gonna figure out my hours so that I can take really good care of you, Analie. I'll bring you breakfast in bed and I'll run out to get pickles and ice cream at midnight. And we'll turn the second bedroom here into the nursery... unless you want to get out of town. Wanna get out of town? I could be a cop anywhere. There's nothing holding us here."

Adán, I thought. *He'll never let us get away.*

Maybe I said it out loud, because Corvi shook his head at me.

"We're even with the witch doctor," he said softly. "It's over. Everything is the way it should be. Just ask the Barretts. They're on their way over right now. All three of them..."

"What?" My voice came out like a wisp of smoke, frail and disappearing into nowhere right before our eyes, barely existing. "What did you say?"

"You heard me," said Corvi, and despite everything, I could hear the tenderness in his voice, and I knew that he loved me. I wanted to scratch his eyes out and push him backwards until he crashed through the window and fell to a crushing and bloody death on the sidewalk below. I wanted to press my mouth against his and then bite his lips off. I wanted to grab that corn silk hair and bring his face down onto my knee with all my might and smash that straight nose and burst every blood vessel in those pale brown eyes. He could see it, looking at me, he could see everything I wanted to do, and he was going to weather it with me, and wait it out, because he loved me.

"Mia came back," he said gently.

My mouth was open, but no words came out. I stared at his face, doing a frantic assessment. He was joking. He had to be joking.

"I don't believe you," I whispered.

"Don't go out of your mind with happiness and relief," Corvi said dryly. He got up cautiously and sat back on the bed, watching me. "A few days ago, she just showed up. Reese nearly had a heart attack, but he called the police and took her to the hospital and she's okay. Really, not a scratch on her. She's home now."

We stared at each other.

Corvi finally smiled again. He had won and he knew it.

Fuck them. Here comes the burning class.

That never changes.

Corvi looked at his watch. "Actually, they're probably gonna ring the buzzer any second, so why don't you get dressed? When Reese called to tell me the good news, you were out like a goddamn light, and now he's worried about you, and he said they were going to stop by with some food. And Mia wants to see you, of course."

Corvi got up and began rummaging around in the drawers for clothes, handing me a white t-shirt and a pair of jeans.

I let him drop them into my lap, I sat unmoving.

"I don't believe you," I said again.

"Ha, I know, baby," Corvi said. "That's kinda why I'm letting 'em come over, so you can see for yourself. Put your arms up," he said, gently pulling off my shirt and replacing it with the new, clean one. "We can tell 'em our good news and you'll give your notice, 'cause I don't want you taking care of anyone else's baby when we've got one of our own on the way. Mia's probably not gonna go back to work anyway, at least not right away. She's gonna get tested for everything under the sun and brain scans and what-have-you, even though she says she doesn't remember a thing. And I don't think that's ever gonna change. She was gone in every possible way." He helped me into my jeans and then, as if on cue, the buzzer rang. Corvi laughed. "Perfect timing," he said, and stood up straight, patting his pockets. He had jeans on, too, and the shirt that said *The Alamo Under Siege*. His blonde hair was, as usual, sticking up in the back. "I'll get the door. You take a deep breath and come on in and join us when you're ready, okay, baby?" The sound of my breathing was the loudest thing in the room. He put his hand on the side of my face. "Hey, take it easy," he said softly. "Just relax, it's all gonna be okay. This really is all for the best. I love you." And then he was gone. I heard him walk quickly to the intercom and then I knew it would be only a minute or two before the doorbell rang... but who would be on the other side of that door? Reese and... who? Not Mia. It couldn't be Mia.

The doorbell did ring, and I heard Corvi open it and greet our guests loudly and cheerfully. The bedroom door seemed to open for me, untouched, and I drifted in the direction of those voices as though I were floating—I couldn't accept the idea that my feet were connected to me and padding across the floor, steering me to the living room. I didn't feel my feet, only motion.

"There she is," I heard Corvi say.

He stepped to the side, and Reese and Mia Barrett were standing right there.

Mia was holding Brook in her arms.

"Analie, you're okay," said Reese, smiling at me happily. He was holding a big ceramic dish with a cover, and he was glowing. I saw a flicker of something in his eyes—an apology, an acknowledgement—and then it was gone and replaced by his broad, creamy, practiced smile.

Even beside Reese's glow, Mia was so radiant she was hard to look at. Her fair skin was peachier than ever, gilded at the edges as though she was standing in front of a perpetual sunrise. Her light hair was longer and fell to her waist in shiny, silken ripples. Had she really always been this beautiful? Brook clung to her, but his head was turned to me and his eyes were wide, deadened, unyielding. His cheeks looked hot. "You may want to stand back," said Reese, still smiling. "Brooky's been a little sick to his stomach, I don't know if he ate something that didn't agree with him or what, but... there's been a lot of throwing up around our place!"

Mia let out a peal of laughter.

"That's how you welcomed Mommy back," she said. "By getting a tummy bug?" Her voice rose in pitch. "'Hi Mommy, I'm so happy to see you, I'm gonna throw up all over you!'"

Reese laughed too.

"Ah, Analie's seen it all before," said Corvi proudly. "She's gonna make a great mother herself, we just need to get over this little rough patch, right, baby?"

It took Reese and Mia a moment to understand.

"Ohhhhh," they both cooed in unison.

"Amazing," said Reese, his smile faltering only slightly, and Mia murmured, "This is such wonderful news." She handed the silent, dead-eyed Brook over to Reese and began to walk towards me with her arms outstretched.

I stiffened as she approached me and pulled me into an embrace, feeling sicker than I'd ever felt in my life.

It was a new kingdom, again.

New ruler. New rules. And the ruler wasn't me. Once I had held the sun and the moon in my hands and rattled them like dice. Now my hands were empty.

Now the only thing I knew was what she was about to say before she said it.

I bowed my head, relinquishing the crown, breathing in a smoky smell that I knew was only for me. Mia's voice was soft against my ear.

Soft and slightly scorched.

"Hi Leelee," she whispered. "It's so good to see you."

About the Author

Luisa Colón is a Brooklyn-based writer and artist who was born and raised in New York City. Her first novel, *Bad Moon Rising*, was published by Cemetery Dance Publications in 2023

Also by Luisa Colón

BAD MOON RISING

In Gravesend, Brooklyn, sixteen-year-old Elodia is an outcast at school, at odds with her father, and longing for her mysteriously absent mother. Lonely and isolated, Elodia knows that something unspeakably terrible has happened to her—she just can't remember what.

Miles away in upstate New York, a young man named Gabriel occupies his time by killing sparrows and searching for his birth parents. Gabriel wants to show them what a good son he can be, well-behaved and helpful and no trouble at all—until a savage betrayal plants an ever-growing seed of revenge within him.

Desperate for the promise of their past lives and future dreams, both Elodia and Gabriel are broken and scarred, their lives shattered. Their wounds run deep—and that kind of damage is irrevocable. Unchangeable. Irreversible.

... Isn't it?

"Twisty and disturbing, *Bad Moon Rising* is an ambitious, moody meditation on the cycles of familial trauma. Luisa Colon's impressive debut is sure to get under your skin."

— Paul Tremblay, author of *The Cabin at the End of the World and A Head Full of Ghosts*

"What a gem. Luisa's debut novel is poignant, spooky, atmospheric, and absolutely gorgeous. Luisa is a name you're going to want to remember."

— Noelle W. Ihli, author of *Ask for Andrea*

"Bad Moon Rising is a clever and compelling page-turner that packs one hell of an emotional punch. It's a poignant exploration of adolescent relationships, and it had me gripped from the first sentence to the superb ending. Luisa Colón is an exceptional new horror writer to watch!"

— Jeremy Bates, author of *Suicide Forest* and *The Sleep Experiment*

www.ingramcontent.com/pod-product-compliance
Lightning Source LLC
Chambersburg PA
CBHW031102020726
47495CB00007B/2012